La Nouvelle Agence
7, rue Corneille - 75006 PARIS
Tél. 01 43 25 85 60
Fax 01 43 25 47 98

THE LANGUAGE NOBODY SPEAKS

Also by Eugene Mirabelli

The Burning Air
The Way In
No Resting Place
The World at Noon

THE LANGUAGE NOBODY SPEAKS

a novel by
Eugene Mirabelli

SPRING HARBOR PRESS

Printed in the United States of America

ISBN 0-935891-02-1 (Clothbound)
ISBN 0-935891-03-X (Paperbound)
Library of Congress Catalog Card Number: 99-60139

Published by Spring Harbor Press in 1999
Spring Harbor Press is part of Spring Harbor, Ltd.,
Box 346, Delmar, New York, 12054.

Jacket and cover design by Ed Atkeson of Berg Design.
Book design by Seagull Graphics.

Spring Harbor Books may be ordered from the publisher.
Box 346, Delmar, New York, 12054.
Add a dollar for postage and handling.
New York State residents add sales tax.

for Bob and Ricardo

THE LANGUAGE NOBODY SPEAKS

1

DO YOU BELIEVE in love at first sight? I first met Erin at a country wedding and wanted her then and forever, but it was almost a year before I saw her again. We recognized each other right off.

Something must have broken loose just as I drove past the capitol building, because when I tried to pull to the right the car shuddered, so I wrenched to the left and skidded around some damn monument, nearly hit a couple of people and scraped to a halt against the curb half a block farther on. I got out and slammed the door and that's when I saw Erin again. She was coming down the sidewalk at a good clip, a newspaper and a leather portfolio under her arm. "Hi, Bart," she said. "What are *you* doing here?"

Neither of us belonged there. She had come up for a job interview and I had driven over for a mathematics conference and now both of us were heading home to different cities — she to New York, me to Boston. I told her my car had broken down, lost its steering just now. "That was you? That was me you ran over at the news stand," she said. She had clear green eyes and looked at me as if I were in the middle of saying something and she was waiting for me to finish. I was afraid she'd get away again and asked her where she was going. "I'm on my way to the station," she told me.

"And I have to find a mechanic," I said. I threw my jacket and tie in the car and locked it. We began walking in the sun. I rolled up my sleeves and we talked about how hot it was. Erin was wearing a trim gray business suit — slender jacket and narrow skirt that whipped and snapped at each brisk step. "I don't mind this," she explained, plucking at the lapel of her jacket. "It's the stockings I hate. But I can't very well go to a job interview bare legged." I was surprised that anything as thin and weightless as a woman's stocking could feel hot, and I said so. She smiled. "You ought to try wearing them some time," she said.

I asked how the interview had gone. They had said they would let her know. "But I don't think I got it. And just as well. I don't care to live here in Albany, not what I've seen of it. Upstate New York is for cows and apples," she said. I wanted to ask her to dinner and was trying to recall how much money I had on me, and she must have sensed my intention for she became alert and wary. I asked what time her train was leaving. She looked at her watch. "Twenty-five minutes," she said. She was sweating and tossed her head nervously now and again, as if to shake the hair from her eyes. We had come to a narrow cobbled street that dropped down to the next avenue and Erin turned into it. Down below you could see the thoroughfare blazing white in the sun, but it was mercifully cool in the alley. We were in the shade when Erin sidestepped into a recessed doorway, pulled up her skirt and unfastened the silvery garter clips and began to roll down the stocking. I went momentarily blind at the sight of those long tense thighs and the tight bulge of white underwear at her crotch. She had rolled down the other stocking and now smoothed her skirt with a single brisk stroke of her palm, stepped into her shoes and resumed walking beside me, her heels making a tap tap tap on the cobbles. "Cooler?" I asked. "Much," she said and slipped the stockings like a wad of gold leaf into her portfolio. I asked her could she take a later train, could she have dinner with me. She said she hoped so, and we came out to the sun at the foot of the alley.

2

THERE WAS a small restaurant a short way up from the station and we went in. The sign had said EAT but place was almost empty. Erin unfolded her train schedule and began looking through it. The solitary and rather dejected couple who had entered just before us turned idly our way and I saw it was Hollis Lord and his wife. I couldn't recall his wife's name and, as a matter of fact, I didn't know Hollis himself very well. He was older than I, a tall lean man who managed a small museum or ran an art gallery, or something like that, back in Boston. "Look who's here," he said, breaking into a smile. And they both said, "Come sit with us, won't you? Yes, join us. Please." That's not what I had had in mind when we came in, but it would be awkward to insist on sitting at a separate table in a place as small and deserted as this. I glanced at Erin who — to my surprise — smiled and refolded her train schedule.

"This is Hollis Lord and his wife —" I began.

"Lida," his wife volunteered, shaking Erin's hand. Lida was in her mid thirties, a handsome woman with a broad face and a mass of vigorous, tawny hair.

"We've met before," Erin told her, holding her hand. "Didn't you have a show in New York about six months ago? An East Side gallery?" Erin asked her. Now I recalled that Lida Lord was an artist of some sort, a painter or sculptor. And, yes, it turned out that she had had an exhibit in the city this past winter and Erin had been at the opening. "This *is* a coincidence," Hollis said, laughing. "A lucky accident, our running into you this way." Frankly, I had had my lucky accident ten minutes ago and this was something else.

We four had the place to ourselves. It was early and none of us was especially hungry, so we ordered salad and talked amiably of this and that. It turned out that Hollis was not directing a small museum or gallery in Boston after all. The trustees for whom he had worked had decided to merge their holdings with those of some other small New England archive and in the process they had eliminated Hollis's job. He had been living in the Berkshires for the past few months, writing a book on nineteenth century British painters. "The morbid ones," Lida explained. I told them I had just come from a mathematics conference, that my car had broken down, and Erin spoke briefly about her job interview with some lobbyists. But it was very clear the Lords believed we had arranged our rendezvous, believed we were lovers on a tryst. I was happy to have them think so — Erin, sitting at my side, let her arm rest against mine on the table, and said nothing to set them straight — and, in fact, the idea seemed to heighten the Lords' obvious pleasure in us.

"What brings you to Albany?" Erin asked them.

Lida abruptly attended to her salad. Hollis looked

glum and said, "That's a sad story."

"We came to see lawyers," Lida said at last, frowning at a slice of tomato on the end of her fork.

"Property," Hollis added a moment later. He looked to Lida as if expecting her to amplify his remark, but she said nothing. "We have a piece of property here in the Berkshires and we have to sell it," he said. "It's nothing elaborate, but we like it. Hate to see it go."

The property — they called it the shack, the studio, the barn — was situated in the gentle Berkshire mountains, equidistant from Boston and New York City. Lida spent a lot of time in New York these days, they told us. Erin asked them outright why they were selling it if they liked it so much. "Money," he said. Lida had paused and was looking at him, apparently as interested as we were in what he was saying. "Money," he said again, agreeably. Lida turned to us and put her hand over Erin's, squeezing it. "But we're not broke yet," she told us with a broad smile.

Lida had an intriguing voice which I can not describe except to say that it sounded dusky, if I can use that word to convey its oddly rough texture, and she spoke with an accent, but so subtly that at first I had taken it as a trick of my ear. Yes, she told us, it was an accent. She was born in Prague, grew up in Trieste and came to this country after the war. After learning that, I thought I saw Slavic accents in the broad bones of her face, her open gestures and large hands. Once in a while she would give my name a full Italian pronunciation, rolling *Bartolomeo* on her tongue. She was about thirty-five, I guessed, and Hollis about forty years old, maybe older, but I found it hard to estimate their ages because of the frank and fraternal way they talked with us, suggesting by everything they said that we were, all of us, at the same point in life. Of course, we were not at the same point and every now and again I felt Lida using a slightly managerial style with us, especially with Erin, but whenever that happened it was countered by Hollis's deference. And above all this I felt their genuine affection, as if they had adopted us on the spot.

Near the end of dinner Hollis asked about the conference I had just attended. I told him it was on topology and didn't say more than that, because in my experience no one really wants to know very much about a math conference. He said he admired mathematicians and had always imagined mathematics as the realm of the absolute, a place you came to when you had penetrated everything else, a place where you could roam utterly free of passion and vice. I knew it would sound impolite if I tried to set him straight. Lida asked me what it was that mathematicians actually did. "Mathematicians solve math problems," I told her. I hadn't intended a flippant answer, but had been distracted by Erin slyly bumping my shoe with her foot again and again.

"Like we did back in school?" Lida asked.

"More or less," I said.

"But where do they come from? Where do the problems come from?" she asked.

"From other mathematicians," I said. Erin was gazing at me with innocent attention, all the while rubbing her bare foot against my ankle as if she had forgotten what she was up to. "Actually, I'm not satisfied by mathematics or by what I do. The whole affair is so insubstantial. I want —" I broke off, afraid to bore everyone with a discourse on my dissatisfaction with the impalpability of mathematics.

"What do you want?" Erin asked me.

I heard something playful or suggestive in the way she asked that question, and while I was searching her face Hollis asked about her job interview and they began talking about that. Lida said she admired writers even more than Hollis admired mathematicians. I had

16

purposely rested my hand on Erin's knee, and now as she talked with Lida she gradually opened her legs for me and I began to slide the cloth up a bit and up a bit more, sinking my hand between her thighs. Just when I felt my hand would melt from the smoothness of her flesh she clamped her knees together, trapped me there. That's the way we were as she leaned forward, her elbows on the table, leaned forward in conversation, saying, "No. I'm not writing now. I'm between jobs." She turned and gave me a brief look, a slight flush on her cheeks. "And I'm not entirely comfortable this way," she said to me, her legs still clamped together. The Lords announced that they had spent far too much time alone with each other — they enjoyed our company, they knew Albany well and they wanted to show us around town. "That would be nice," Erin said. I agreed. She parted her legs and I withdrew my hand.

At the restaurant door Erin turned to me for an instant, saying quietly, "I can catch a train back to the city tomorrow." Then she turned away and I followed her out to join Hollis and Lida. We had split the dinner bill and I knew I had enough cash on hand to pay for a small double in a cheap hotel, but I had never done anything like that, had always thought it a sleazy thing to do, and the prospect made me uncomfortable. I turned it round and round in my head while the others walked along debating whether the air was cooler than before or only seemed that way. Hollis told us that the street was on the flood plain, almost on a level with the Hudson River, and that's why it was so hot and humid here. When we came to their automobile, he unlocked the doors and we rolled down all the windows and let the car stand open at the curb for a few minutes, hoping that the interior would cool off. It was a Jaguar, sedate and sleek, but oddly marred by a school of small minnow-size scratches along the side and a deep crease across one of the graceful front mudguards. Erin said she had never been in a Jaguar. It had leather upholstery and the doors snapped shut with a muffled *click*, sounding not so much like a vault as a rich lady's compact. Hollis drove past the train station, informing us that this street was called Broadway and this next one — here we rounded a corner and headed smoothly up hill — was called State Street. The sidewalks were almost deserted. We continued to drive up hill. "What's the chateau?" Erin asked. And, in fact, the huge gray stone structure looming above us with its massive windows, its steep slate roof with that iron picket fence perched on the ridge — it did look like a fancy French palace. That was the State Capitol Building, Lida told her. Then we passed a broad cataract of stone steps and I saw a monument off to the right and spied the street where I had parked my busted VW.

Hollis pulled to the curb and we all got out to look around. Lida pointed out City Hall (clock tower, red tile roof) and some other buildings. In back of the Capitol Building we came to an empty park, a desolate rectangle of grass punctuated by barren flower beds, and at the other end stood a huge office building which must have been the tallest structure in upstate New York. We trudged along but seemed to make no progress, maybe because we were creeping up a slight incline or because the oversize buildings obliterated our sense of distance, stranding us on a walkway much longer than it looked. Friday night traffic went tearing by on the avenue. We went on and on beside an endless row of gigantic columns which, Hollis informed us, comprised the largest colonnade in the world or something like that. I began to wonder what the hell we were doing here. Erin and I let ourselves drift further and further behind the Lords and began to talk about that country wedding where we had met so many months ago, and why we had not been able to get in touch with each other. Both of us had tried.

18

"I asked a couple of people after you left," she said, squinting into the distance and pushing her hair back. "They told me you were involved with someone."

I laughed. "No. Not involved. Just passing time." I told her how I had talked to my cousin and she had said she'd find out what she could. "And all she found out was you were going to get married," I said.

"It wasn't serious," Erin said with a shrug. We walked along in silence for a few moments, and I supposed that she was thinking about the same things I was thinking about, and wondering if this was going to be serious or a waste of time or what. Anyway, I couldn't help myself and even if I had foreseen the parched sexual frenzy we four were waltzing toward, I couldn't have stopped. Lida and Hollis had slowed and finally come to a halt several paces ahead of us and were not sightseeing at all, but simply standing there half-turned our way, glancing at us now and again, keeping a watchful eye on us while talking to each other in a quiet, serious way. I suppose that's when this cannibal adventure began — with them looking at us, sizing us up, weighing the possibilities.

"I think they believe we're orphans," Erin said, smiling.

"Where do you want to spend the night?" I asked.

"That's up to you," she said. "Anywhere is all right with me. We could spend the night just walking around if you want." Her eyes were steady, the green somewhat darker than it had been earlier in the afternoon, and I felt a surge of desire in my chest so strong it was painful.

"That might be better than what I had in mind," I said. "I can't afford a halfway decent hotel room."

Lida and Hollis were sauntering back toward us, casual and at ease, as if they had figured out something and come to a decision.

"I have some money —" Erin had begun to say, but she saw the Lords were close and broke off.

Lida said we should all get in the car and drive over to the Governor's mansion and then up to a park on the high side of town. And that's what we did. Erin and I were going to spend the night together, but frankly I was unsure how best to go about it and Erin seemed to have no plan or preference, either. So it was easy to drive around with the Lords a bit longer, all the while trying to figure out exactly what to do. Hollis swung the Jaguar from the curb and we crossed some avenues and bumped slowly down a patched side street past the Governor's residence. The house was situated up hill from the street, a dark red brick structure which, Hollis remarked, looked like a nineteenth century textile mill with a few porches added on. An old artillery piece stood on the front lawn, ready to demolish the row of houses across the street. "Do you suppose the cannon will protect him from the colorful neighbors?" Lida asked. The neighborhood was a dreary brick slum. We began driving up hill again and eventually we came level into Washington Park. The park road made slow meandering loops that took us over a few hillocks and past a couple more monuments, including a big group statue of Moses and a handful of his followers on some rocks, their arms upraised — "They're lost and they're arguing which way to go next," Hollis said. — then the road curved down to a pond which was spanned at one end by an old-fashioned iron bridge, and thence around about to the street. We drew up at the margin of the park and got out of the car. The air was mild. People were sauntering about — a couple of young women had put a radio on a bench and were dancing together, singing along softly to the music, and a few paces beyond them a man lay on his back with his arms and legs flung out, a newspaper folded beneath his head, and here came a little girl seated happily on her father's shoulders, her legs straddling his neck and her feet in his hand-stirrups as he walked slowly across the grass with his wife — ordinary people enjoying the indolence of a Friday evening. I could feel the moments slip away and I knew that if I didn't choose a place for the two of us to spend the night I'd be as lost as Moses. I put my arm around Erin.

"Why don't you two come to Saratoga with us?" Lida suggested.

"Oh, we couldn't do that," Erin said, laughing.

"Remember my broken down car," I said. "Erin and I can't go anywhere."

"We're like you, we hadn't planned to go to Saratoga when we got up this morning," Hollis explained. "But it's beautiful, this time of year."

"Have you ever been there?" Lida asked us.

No, we hadn't

"It's an old fashioned spa. That's what it used to be famous for, the mineral waters. And it has a lovely race course," she told us. "Do you like horse racing?"

Neither Erin nor I had ever been to the races.

"It's so lovely, the horses, the colors that the jockeys wear, the silks. And there's a spa where you can get a blissful massage," she added, turning to Erin with a broad smile.

"Let's get some coffee," Hollis said, touching me gently on the arm. "We hadn't planned to go to Saratoga, but with four of us it seems just exactly right," he added.

We sat at a tiny cafe table with our knees bumping and talked about Saratoga. It was impossible plan, and I said so. Saratoga was thirty or forty miles north of us and it would take time to drive there, even in the Jaguar, and when we arrived we wouldn't have a place to stay. But Hollis said the place had been a summer resort for a couple of hundred years and was full of hotels. Lida told us there were elegant old wrecks decorated with crystal and brass and mirrors, and there were modern ones with everything up to date. So we could go there on the spur of the moment and find suitable rooms and, as a matter of fact, the Lords had a friend who managed a hotel in Saratoga and they always stayed at that one for next to nothing and so could we, as their friends. I said I could pay for our rooms. "Whatever you want, of course," Hollis assured me. "It's just that we like that particular hotel because it's well kept and has beautiful grounds. And it's less expensive than anything down here." I looked to Erin. She gave me a calm green gaze, assenting to any plan I might come up with, as if worldly Bart knew more about assignations than innocent Erin did. "All right. Why not?" I said.

"Yes," said Erin. "Why not?"

Lida squeezed my wrist and turned to Hollis who went to a phone to book our hotel rooms, then we all drove downtown to the side street where I had left my car. I pulled out my overnight bag, took my jacket and necktie from the front seat where I had tossed them a decade ago. A solitary sign said NO PARKING FROM HERE TO CORNER, but my broken down VW looked safe for the night in the middle of the block. I locked the doors and walked back to the Jaguar with my gear. Erin and Lida had gone off to a drugstore to buy cigarettes or something and now they returned and we settled into the leather seats and began the drive to Saratoga.

3

AT FIRST we were all talking together, but Erin and I were in the back seat and after a while we simply watched the city dwindle and fall away. We passed over the Mohawk river, a stretch of light like a melted mirror between the darkening banks, and went up through some small towns and into the countryside. On our left the sky was gold with streaks of red, and on our right it was violet and then, between one moment and the next, the darkness flowed up and covered us. I reached for Erin just she turned to me, passing her arm through mine. Hollis and Lida were in quiet conversation, their faces softly illuminated by the small light of the dashboard. The car hummed along and I was filled with a blurred emotion which I couldn't find a name for, no more than I could correctly name an old dance tune that might come into my head. The feeling had something to do with Erin and me sitting in the back with the other couple up front, moments recalled from rides homeward late at night with my parents up front while I drifted on a sleep made delicious by the sound of their murmurous voices over the steady thrum of the tires, but it took even more from other nights not in childhood, took from — it came back in a rush — those high school double-dates with me and Deborah in the dark back seat, Dave Lombardi and Sue Griffin in the front, riding home from a dance at Norumbega Park. Maybe Erin was thinking about dates in a back seat, too, because now she looked at me and unbuttoned her jacket and I lifted my hand against her breast, kissing her. It was quiet in the car and my heart was banging in my chest. She dropped her hand inside my groin, her fingers seeking me through the trousers, sliding and pressing. Lida turned around and watched us — saw Erin's hand contracting slowly on the bulging cloth, now opening, now closing — then she smiled and turned back to strike up a quiet conversation with Hollis. Lida's indulgent look had set my head on fire, I yanked Erin's blouse from her skirt and slid my hand inside, against her bra. Then the car slowed, we wrenched apart and peered out the windows at the woods opening up for our headlights. Erin surreptitiously dabbed at her sweaty upper lip with the lapels of her blouse. Hollis turned from the roadway onto a gravel drive that took us past a long white facade with broad sagging steps and a blaze of illuminated windows. It was one of those elegant wrecks Lida had told us about. While waiting at the reception desk I glanced through a wide doorway and saw rooms opening onto still more distant rooms, as if I were looking down a telescope the wrong way. "This used to be a private home. Can you imagine it?" Lida said. We signed in, got our keys, and went up a thinly carpeted stairway to our hall. The Lords said, "See you in the morning. The lobby, around nine," and turned in.

In our room I unlocked what I took to be our closet door and faced a second door, that one without a knob. I had seen this makeshift arrangement before in old fashioned tourist homes and country inns. The second door, which could be opened only from the other side, went to the next room, the Lords' room. I shut our door, slid the bolt. Erin dropped her leather portfolio on the desk, I put my overnight bag on the bureau and we fell on each other, fell rolling on the carpet. "Listen," Erin gasped. "You remember how we talked at the wedding that afternoon?"

"Yes, of course, yes." I rolled over her.

She rolled over me. "I want to go on that way," she said, out of breath. "I want to pick up where we left off. I want to talk —"

I cut in, saying, "Do you want to talk down here or on the bed or outside or —"

"Outside. Yes, outside."

She sprang up, straightening her skirt. Actually, I hadn't really meant it when I said outside, but I stood and tucked myself down as much as I could and we stumbled out to the hall. The direction we had come from would lead us past the Lords' door, so we went the other way. Around a corner at the far end of the hall we found a narrow stairway and went down it, descending to a long corridor that lead us to the reception room. We went across the faded carpet and out the double doors to the night. It was too dark to see the grounds. The invisible lawn felt soft underfoot, the air was sweet with the scent of pine and the stars looked like they had been freshly washed and set out to dry. We talked about constellations and hunted for Leo and, not finding it, turned to look for Virgo, which we may or may not have found.

"You remember our conversation?" Erin asked. I knew she meant our conversation a year ago, and I said sure I remembered it.

"You remember when I said no one ever truly understands anyone else?" she continued. "Because it's almost impossible to tell the truth about yourself to anyone else, because you know the difference between the words and what you feel, and it's certainly impossible for anyone to understand what you mean, because the same words say different things to different people. And you said it doesn't matter —"

"I said it doesn't matter?"

"Yes," she insisted. "You said the more precise the words get, the less they say about the heart of things, until —"

"I said that?"

"Yes. The more precise the words get, the less they say, until at last they become mathematics."

I laughed. "And say the least about the least. I remember now."

"What I want to know is, why doesn't it matter?"

"It doesn't matter, because people can understand each other well enough with ordinary words," I said.

We walked in silence for a while. There was only starlight to see by and the air so black that Erin's face seemed almost illusory. "Well," Erin said quietly. "For once in my life I'd like to make myself clear to someone. — You, I mean. I want to make myself clear to you."

"You have," I told her. "Or at least you've started to. I like you so much."

"How do I know you really know who I am! How do I know it's *me* you want?"

"Everything you say tells me who you are, every breath and gesture. You speak and you —"

"Listen," she said abruptly. "When I began fooling around I wanted love. It was love, love, love and more love, I wanted. Then I outgrew that and what I wanted was sex, just sex with nothing else. I certainly didn't want to have to listen to some solemn young man telling me he loved me, just so we could get to it. Not a relationship, not a commitment, just plain clean and uncomplicated sex is what I was after. And I'm so damned tired of it. I don't want another empty —"

I knew she was going to say fuck and I touched my hand to her mouth, stopping her. "Neither do I," I told her.

"I mean it," she said, taking my hand in hers. "I don't want —"

"I know," I said, cutting her off.

"I don't want another empty fuck," she said quietly.

"I know. I know. And neither do I."

But I wondered how we were going to get from here to bed together, because I badly wanted to get there and I felt she did, too. We had come to a grove of pine, the trunks like huge pillars of thickened darkness. The ground rose unevenly beneath a slippery carpet of pine needles and we slowed almost to a halt, let go each other's hand and began walking cautiously into the blind shadow beneath those black boughs. There was not even the starlight.

"And maybe I have trouble making myself clear, making myself known, because there is nothing, really nothing here to know," she told me.

"How can you say that?"

"You think you know me?"

"No. But I know I want to," I said.

She didn't answer. I couldn't see her at all, but I hoped her silence meant she accepted what I had said, meant she believed me. We walked close in the dark, so close that I listened for her breath and felt her presence — the shape and warmth of her flesh — where we almost touched, as if the night had absorbed her clothing and left her naked.

"Now this is what I call dark. Let's try to find our way back," she muttered.

I heard a note of anxiety in her voice, so we turned and began walking through the pines toward the hotel.

"I suppose this is what's it's like to have no body," I said. "To be just a disembodied mind, a voice, words."

"Oh, no, no. Not at all," she objected.

I laughed. "You *know* what it's like to be bodiless?"

"Yes. No! I mean, I always *imagined* it to be just the opposite of this. I always thought of being bodiless as being light, radiant white light. Not this, this black, this nothingness. You would see light. I'm certain about it."

"How could you see light if you didn't have eyes? You would have to have eyes if you didn't have a body."

"Are you making fun of me?"

"I'm taking you seriously."

"Because I was only a kid when I thought about it. I wanted to transcend the flesh, to be a pure spirit. Actually, I haven't given it much thought since I was sixteen. But *this* — This is like some pagan notion of being dead. When I said bodiless I didn't mean dead, you know."

"This is like being dead before the Resurrection," I said.

"Well. Yes. Maybe," she said tentatively, thinking about it.

"Because after the Resurrection we get our bodies back and can see each other."

She laughed and said my name, "Bart, Bart, Bart. Tell me the truth. Do you think it's possible to know some one without knowing that person's body?"

I thought about it, turned it around and around, and the answer was always yes and no. "No, not really. — What about you?"

"What about me? What do you mean?"

"What do you think? Do you think it's possible to know a person without —"

"Oh, I suppose you're right," she said irritably.

"No. Tell me what *you* think."

"It's obvious I feel the same way you do. I'm not an angelic spirit. I quit when I was sixteen, remember? Of course I want to know bodies. But I think — I mean, I feel —"

"What?"

"I know we're more than just words, I know we're flesh and blood."

"And bones and nerves," I added.

"And bones and nerves and skin and so on. Our bodies are as important as our words. I know all that. Our bodies are another language. Right? Our bodies are another language, but no one speaks it. People just shout at each other and make noise and call it making love."

We had come out from under the pines and were crossing the dark lawn in silence. I said, "I hope you're not fed up with it." And Erin said, "On the contrary, I'm starved." When I put my arm around her shoulders she turned to kiss me. In the dark I got the jolt of her mouth on my mouth, and when I kissed her throat there was the heat and taste and scent of her flesh, making my head spin. We were standing near the shadowy bulk of some old fashioned lawn ornament — a huge cast iron bird bath or fountain or something like that — and there was a bench beside it so we sat down. Erin asked did she need to know much about the person I had been only friends with. I said no, which was the truth, and told her how we had gotten to know each other because we lived in the same apartment house, and that we had gone to bed together only if we both happened to be lonely on the same night, which almost never happened, and that was the truth, too. "Well, I thought I was going to marry him," Erin told me. I asked had he been nice, and Erin said he had been much nicer than nice, and that's why she had thought she was going to marry him. "But there was no way I was as nice as he was. And after a while I began to feel like a fraud," she added. We talked about weddings and about the starry coincidences that had brought us to the same wedding, and talked about our families and whether people who came from Ireland and Sicily were more alike than not, because they came from island countries, talked about how many uncles and aunts we had and so on. The glowing windows of the hotel had gone dark, this one and that one, like candles being blown out, and now a whole row along the bottom went dark in a gust all at once. We talked about a hundred different things and I knew for certain what I had only guessed at before, that we could talk to each other about anything — about Kepler and his ingenious attempts to fit the universe into a mystical system of mathematics, or about some book that Erin read where a character lives for ages and even changes sex as the story goes along. And we might have talked about Hollis and Lida, except that we had nothing to tell each other about them. Erin looked at the stars and remarked on how far the Big Dipper had swung around. "Did you ever wonder why the sky is so dark? I mean, if there are all those zillions of stars out there we should see a star wherever we look and the sky should be blazing with starlight," she said. By then the night was stilled, for even the crickets had ceased chirping and had fallen asleep, and we walked back to the hotel.

While Erin was taking a shower I tore off my clothes and sorted through my overnight bag to rediscover what I had brought with me. There was one fresh shirt, a clean pair of shorts, my shaving kit, a page of program notes from the conference, two offprints of my stale article on discontinuities in certain equations relating to physical processes, my checkbook and a brown paper bag with yesterday's soiled laundry. I hoped I could cash a check here at the hotel tomorrow morning. Erin was brushing her teeth and I guessed she must have bought the tooth brush just before we ducked into the car for the drive up here. Her portfolio was open on the desk and I could see a small box printed with blue flowers and an uncut cellophane packet of nylon stockings. She came from the bathroom in her cotton briefs. The sun had tanned her flesh to a light gold — topaz color, actually — leaving her breasts startlingly white. While I was gazing at her, her eyes wavered and she turned her head aside, glanced away at the wall or floor, the color coming to her cheeks, her nipples stiffening. She tossed her hair back and faced me again. I wanted to say something to put us at ease, but couldn't think what. "Don't go away, I'll be right back," was all I said, stepping past her. She turned, smiling. "No rush. I'll save your place," she told me. I turned on the shower hot and hard, let it drive on me while the room dissolved into steam, then I hopped out, dried off and stepped through the door with a towel around my waist. Erin met me in the middle of the room, lifting her arms to embrace me. We stayed together that way, I don't know how long, not long. For she sank down on her knees and after a silent look into my eyes, lowered her head and took that beastly plum into her mouth so tenderly that I groaned. Then she lay back upon the bed with her hands on my shoulders while I kissed her breasts and her belly and went down to breathe the floral scent she had put on her wild hair, and with her hands on my head I went deeper down, feeling her heat on my cheek, tasting her taste. What can I recall after so many years? When I moved into her I felt myself entering the tender petals of an opening flower, the dark rose red or empurpled pink of a tropical sea anemone, clasping with gentle solace.

4

THE NEXT MORNING I pulled up the shades and looked out the windows to see where we had been transported to the night before, a fresh green landscape (green pines, wide green fields, faraway green hills) with everything clean and bright under a blue sky. It felt right to find our new selves in a new place. Erin had come up behind me and had slipped her bare arms under mine and around my naked chest, pressing her warm breasts to my back, kissing my neck. After a short while we threw ourselves onto the bed and made love in a rush. Later we went down to the front lobby to cash a check and meet Hollis and Lida — Erin phoned her apartment mates in New York, told them not to worry about her absence — then we drove a mile or so to the center of town. It happened that Erin was talking with Lida when we got into the Jaguar, so those two sat together in the back and I sat up front with Hollis. And I thought it was better that way — Erin and I not sitting together — because my arteries were still so flooded with her from an hour ago that I had trouble seeing or listening to anyone else. Now as we drove along I tried to pay attention to Hollis who was telling us about some Irish immigrant who had made a pile of money cutting lumber in the Adirondaks and how he had built himself a gingerbread mansion that eventually became the hotel we were staying at. Lida pointed out a couple of spas and Hollis informed us that Saratoga's full official name was actually Saratoga Springs and that people still came from all over to drink the water and even to bathe in it. I noticed the town wasn't very big. There was a single wide avenue straight up the middle with some narrow streets going off to the left and right and, as Hollis said, it was mostly hotels and restaurants and shops for people on vacation. To tell the truth, the place had a sad look about it.

We found a parking space and walked down one of the side streets to a cheerful little hole in the wall and had pancakes and bacon and all the mugs of coffee we could drink. While we were eating, Hollis talked about some of the bigger antique hotels up on the main street and said that he would walk us through a couple of the lobbies. "But only if you want to, only if you want to," he added with a smile. "The Victorian era may not fascinate you as much as it fascinates me." Erin asked about all those people who had come to Saratoga and what had they done for entertainment once they got here. "They arranged dances, they went to the race track, they carried on," Lida told her. "It was better than the city in August."

"And people still do this?" Erin asked.

"Oh, yes," Lida assured her. "They do this all the time in Europe, you know. The French, the Italians, the Swiss, the Germans, they go to spas. They say it's good for the liver. Of course, in Europe everyone claims to be suffering from a bad liver. No matter what their symptoms are, it's the liver."

"But do they actually get better? If it's only mineral water —"

Lida laughed. "I have no idea. But if you go off to a nice hotel where they prepare all your meals and where all you do is bathe and get massaged each morning and maybe carry on a flirtation in the afternoon, yes, you will certainly feel better than if you had stayed in the city and worked."

Erin and Lida were sitting side by side across the table from Hollis and me, and whenever I looked too long at Erin I would lose hold of what was being said and drift into a reverie of a few hours ago. Erin's face looked shamelessly naked to me, the smooth workmanship of the lids, the detail of the iris, her mouth, those high cheeks. I knew I saw her this way only because we had just finished making love, but at the same time I felt that Lida and Hollis must see the nakedness, too, and despite the shower we had taken this morning I feared we still showed signs of it on our bodies, her inner oils and scents on my hands and mouth, my sticky milk glistening on her breast. Now I came back to the conversation because Erin said something about wanting to get out of her business suit, wanting to buy a skirt and blouse this morning. She was wearing yesterday's blouse unbuttoned part way down with the collar spread against the gray jacket lapels. It looked fine to me but, as she said, it was a business suit and she wanted to feel on vacation.

Lida said she knew a couple of good shops that might have what Erin wanted. "And I happen to have some things with me, some jerseys and light pullovers that might fit you," she added. "By the way, do you like old fashioned clothes? There's a wonderful shop here that sells antique clothing — camisoles, corsets with stays, lacy slips — it's lovely, some of it, actually beautiful." For emphasis she had put her hand on Erin's wrist, and now she reached up with the other hand and gently swept some loose strands of hair back from Erin's cheek, tucking them behind her ear while Erin remained as still as an attentive child, gazing into the older woman's eyes. "And you'd look beautiful in one of those white summer dresses," Lida told her quietly, smiling. "You *are* beautiful."

After breakfast Erin and Lida went off to hunt for a blouse or something, and Hollis came along with me while I got a pair of socks. Actually, I bought a striped jersey and a pair of under shorts, as well as socks, then we walked back to the car to wait for Erin and Lida. The main street was wide and was flanked by buildings from the 1800s, ugly boxes of stone and masonry with massive keystones over each door and window, and there were no trees anywhere. "This is Broadway," Hollis informed me. "And it used to be lined with tall wineglass elms, many of them a hundred years old, that met overhead and shaded the entire street." Erin and Lida didn't turn up right away and when we looked down the sidewalk we still couldn't see them anywhere, so Hollis wrote a note and put it on the car dashboard, saying that we had taken a walk to Congress Park. While we were walk-

34

ing idly along Hollis began to tell me about the gamblers and women who used to come here.

Hollis was an amiable man and I was happy that we had decided to go along with him and Lida. I still couldn't tell whether he was in his early or his late forties, and for a while I tried to match him with other of my acquaintances who looked about as old as he did, but it seemed silly so I stopped. He was my height or maybe a shade taller. He was lean as a whip, stood straight and had a way of tilting his head back ever so slightly, and that may have made him appear taller to me. His hair was a bit longer than was stylish and it was black, except at his temples where it was feathered with white. He had gray eyes and I suppose you could say they were sad, but he was so animated when he talked that you rarely glimpsed the melancholy. And certainly he did enjoy talking. While we drifted along he not only told me anecdotes about raffish visitors to the place, but also pointed out architectural details on the buildings on the other side the street. His favorite was an old gray hotel with a big porch across the front and tall thin decorated pillars that went up three stories to where a roof jutted out. The facade had heavy ledges and brackets and a lot of busted cast iron trim and, frankly, the whole thing gave me a headache to look at it. Hollis said that in the early 1800s one of the first Saratoga hotels had a porch and wood pillars that went up three stories, and that for the next hundred years most of the public building here were made that way. People would dress up in their finery and promenade the length of Broadway on those long hotel piazzas, while other guests sat in rocking chairs on the upper galleries and kept an eye on the parade of splendid coaches. Those places were huge. One of the hotels had a hundred waiters and a dining hall which could seat a thousand guests. The United States Hotel went for a half mile if you walked around it, and it looked like an entire city block that had been lifted from Paris and set down in Saratoga, complete with private dining salons and dark rosy silken chambers where anything might go on. And the Grand Union, the biggest in the world, had a three-acre park with fountains and shade trees tucked inside its courtyard. People came from as far away as Georgia or the Carolinas and once they got here every group mingled with all the others, so this was a grand place to meet all sorts of people from the richest to the poorest, and to dance or to flirt or have an affair or to gamble at cards or to drink or have a fine meal, bet on horses or play three-in-a-bed with elegant prostitutes. Now all that was left on Broadway from that era was this big collapsing thing with the ugly pillars and the rickety galleries and a smaller hotel huddled next to it on the corner, but Hollis knew so much and told it so well that I actually began to feel something for those bygone people.

When we got to the margin of the park we turned and headed back to the car and arrived there just as Erin and Lida were reading our note. Erin looked up and saw me and smiled — it felt like punch in the chest, she was so beautiful. She had an armful of packages and was wearing a new blue-and-white striped jersey. I said, "I bought one like that." And I pulled it out of the car to show her. The Lords were amused, but Erin was truly delighted at the coincidence and took it as a good augury. Lida said they had been delayed by playing with the expensive clothes in a tack shop, one of those places that sold elegant boots and riding gear for women. Then we all talked at once and came to the conclusion that we would go to the antique clothing store so that Lida could try dressing Erin in old fashioned clothes while Hollis and I judged the results — just for the fun of it.

The shop was down one of the side streets and its window displayed a pair of old dressmaker's dummies, one in a gown from the 1870s which was tight as a glove, except at the rear where it had a bustle and flounces, and the other in a dress from around 1910, I guess, an hourglass with a cataract of lace down the front. It was a shabby little place, shaped like a shoe box inside, run by a middle-aged woman who sat on a stool behind the counter, sewing and glancing longingly out the window. She sold not only antique clothing but some newly made copies, too. And that was good, because the old stuff had faded, leaving the colors so dingy that they appeared to be compounded with dust. Lida and Erin swept up a couple of dresses and went into the changing room — actually, it wasn't a room but just a back corner of the shop with a drape hanging across it on a wire. We could hear them talking in low voices, Lida helping her with buttons, murmuring at one point, "What do you bathe in? Your skin is like satin."

"Dolphin's milk," Erin said, dismissing the compliment. "I bathe in dolphin's milk."

"Is that what men call it nowadays?" Lida said, beginning to laugh. "So, so, so, so, so. This is beautiful, too, but you must tuck it in." She had a low, rippling laugh.

I was beginning to get aroused but felt I was eavesdropping, so I walked to the front of the shop and looked out the window to distract myself. Hollis smiled at me as if we were about to play a prank, then raised his voice and called to the women, "Come out, come out, or we'll come in and commit a public nuisance!" They came out and I was startled by the strangeness. Both had put on old fashioned clothing and it had transformed them into women familiar and unknown at the same time, as if they were peeping out at us through a mask. It was oddly fascinating to look at Erin in this or that garment, for when she wore them you could begin to see where the allure and seductiveness of those old styles lay. Lida pointed out that those dresses were designed to be worn over tightly laced corsets, but Erin didn't need a corset and I didn't want to hang around while she took the time to get up in all that rigmarole. One thing I thought looked especially nice was not a dress at all but a chemise, a white under-thing which, when Erin wore it, looked like a cool summer dress, a simple shift made of cotton with a tiny bit of lace here and there. Lida said, "Ah, I knew it — beautiful, beautiful and more beautiful!" then she adjusted the shoulder straps and lifted a thick strand of hair back from Erin's forehead, her strong hands caressing so tentatively you might think she feared burning her fingers on Erin's cheeks. "Very, very nice," said Hollis. Lida wanted Erin to wear the dress to the track that afternoon, but Erin simply laughed and said she didn't have the money for it. "And what would I do with it in the city?" she added, ducking behind the curtain to change. I could see it was on the tip of Lida's tongue to say that she, Lida, would pay for it, but she knew that Erin wouldn't permit it, so she bit her lip and shrugged. "Maybe I'll get something for myself," she said, looking to Hollis. He smiled back at her. "Sure. Why not?"

While we were walking back to the car I began to tell Erin some of the anecdotes that Hollis had told me about the hotels on Broadway. Lida said, "Ah, Hollis has been giving you one of his lectures." But I said no, not a lecture, not at all. "Did he tell you the potato chip was invented here?" Lida asked.

"That's in the lecture about Lake Saratoga," Hollis said amiably. "George Crum was the chef over there."

Erin asked was he joking or what. Then Hollis told us the story about the half-breed chef who sliced the first potato chips, and he talked about the dinners a hundred years ago when the meadows all around were filled with pheasant and the streams packed with trout. He interrupted himself to say, "Let's go over to the Kayadeross-eras. I'll show you the lobby." So we crossed the street to that sad hotel with the long piazza and the sagging galleries and went in. It was as if we had walked into the gray space of an old tintype, into one of those cheap photographs from the 1880s where the touch-up artist has washed the gray faces with pink watercolor and daubed gold paint on all the rings and brooches. The owners had capped the gas pipes — little stumps stuck out of the wall and ceiling — and had thrust electric wires and electric light bulbs into the gas bowls, and on the front desk they had set a Bell telephone with a crooked length of brown, cloth-covered wire that ran up to a black box on the wall, but that was just about it for changes. There were swagged gray velvet drapes, curlicue brack-ets and wood knobs, and the faint odor of musty uphol-stery. Hollis said it was a fine example and was glad the dark clutter had been left as is, but Erin and I felt op-pressed by it. "It makes a nice setting for those old-fash-ioned clothes we were looking at," he said. "And the things that went on in these rooms have a certain power to arouse our interest." It was strange when we left, to push open the doors with their ground glass panes and to step out to Broadway with the elms gone, the sun beat-ing down and the cars driving along in our own era.

5

THAT AFTERNOON we went to the races. By then Erin and I were not at all surprised to see that the club house at the track was a vast wood structure from the last century, a long multitiered building with a sweeping roof line of peaks and gables, topped by flag poles. I had no idea how other race tracks were sited, but this one looked as if the neighbors had simply cleared a flat green field amid the trees and laid out the oval course to settle a wager as to whose horse could run fastest. We pushed our way through the crowd by the edge of the track and watched the horses come around in a wild pounding rush, the jockeys clinging to their backs like demonic goblins whipping them on. The four of us put bets on the early races, then sat in the stands and saw our horses fade or pull up lame. Later in the afternoon we began to talk about leaving, about when we were going back to Albany. The sky was blue with a few clean puffy white clouds and the air was warm and we were having a wonderful time — none of us wanted to go. I needed to get my broken down car into a garage for repairs, and Erin needed to catch a train to New York City. The Lords said that any time was fine for them. We have no plans. It's up to you two, they said. "We'd love to take you home with us," Lida said, smiling.

"At least we'll have a nice drive back to Albany with you two," Hollis said.

"Do you have to go back today?" Lida asked us.

"There's always tomorrow," Hollis suggested.

But Erin and I agreed that we ought to go back today. We left the Lords in the grandstand and went out to the grounds to be alone with each other in the crowd.

"I like them," Erin told me.

"They like us."

"I know. I've never me a woman so fond of me who wasn't obnoxious. But Lida's different, Lida's surprising. I really like her."

I told Erin how Hollis had told me about Europeans building with stone and Americans building with wood, and about the forests that used to cover the land around here, about immigration and the Western Frame and industrial development and millwork techniques — all to explain a bit of wood trim. "He's interested in everything," I said.

The track was located at the edge of a green woods, and the grounds stretched out to long lawns and shade trees with pavilions, here and there, selling cold drinks. We walked a meandering path around the other couples, around an old man (check suit and bow tie) seated in a wheelchair studying his racing form, around some ancient women in large floppy hats who seemed to have motored up from a tea dance, past a man with his baby in his arm and a diaper bag over his shoulder, his racing sheet in hand, through a party of women with brassy hair and dark glasses, and around a tight clump of men with binoculars hanging on their chests and every pocket sprouting a sheaf of paper.

"I've never seen such an assortment," I said.

We had paused in the shade of a huge maple to gaze across the trampled lawn to the red-striped tents that poked up through the crowd. Erin said, "Some of the women look so elegant and some look so tawdry and I can never tell which ones are the whores."

"Those nice old ladies over there," I said, glancing at the old women in white gloves and floppy hats. "Certainly they —"

"Retired whores, expensive ones," she said briskly.

I smiled. "Well, it's a flashy crowd. But I think those are socialites from Albany."

Erin laughed and shrugged her shoulders. "Yeah. Well. Most of the flash and glitter is just to distract you or to cover up something. Or it's used to make a fake self." She tilted her head slightly toward the woman wandering past us in black leather jeans, black eye shadow and pink lipstick, a brimming paper cup in one hand and a cigarette in the other. "Like that one," she said.

"A nun on vacation?" I ventured.

"Exactly!" Erin smiled triumphantly.

"Is this what you write about?"

"No, never. I write about whatever I'm paid to write about. I write speeches for lobbyists. I write articles about dairy products and water resources. They pay me, I write it. I suppose that makes me another kind of whore."

I objected, but Erin went on.

"Oh, it's true. Some women fake orgasms and others fake an entire self. Most women keep the inner self hidden. Especially from the men they go to bed with," she added.

I looked at her, wondering how to take that last bit. She looked back at me with a clear, unrelenting gaze and calmly drew that fallen strand of hair from her cheek and tucked it back of her ear, still gazing straight at me. "What —" I began.

"Don't men do the same thing?" she said, flushing. "Tell me the truth."

"I've known some bogus men, sure. But as for me, I haven't faked a thing. Not with you, anyway. And how could you think so?"

The color seemed to drain from her cheeks, then flood back in a rush. "All I meant," she said hastily. "I meant it could happen without your doing it on purpose. You can be one true self today and a wholly different true self tomorrow. People change. It happens."

"The inner man and the outer man have been the same since I met you. I've never felt more myself in my life."

"But you can't promise that you'll be the same to-morrow. No one can."

"Because I may die tomorrow."

She winced. "Don't say that."

"I may change my mind about a lot of things but not about you. You know how I feel about you and if you want me to say it —"

"Don't say it!" she cried, cutting me off. "No. Wait! Say whatever you want, whatever you mean."

But now I veered away. "How did we get on this? Why are we talking about the true inner self, for God's sake? — Are you faking now or what?"

She wiped her upper lip with the back of her wrist. "My trouble is I don't fake well at all. My trouble is," she began and then broke off. "Look, I've known you for two and a half days if we count that day at the wed-ding. My trouble is I don't know if I can survive without you."

I looked at her — those sea-green eyes, that mouth, the fallen strand of hair — amazed that she could feel that way about me. "What ever made you think I could leave you?" I asked her. "Come on. Let's keep walk-ing."

So we walked here and there on the grounds outside the track, knowing that the time to leave was passing even as we spoke. Neither of us brought up the business of getting back to Albany or getting the car repaired or getting a train back to New York City. I don't know how long we walked, but the crowd in the grandstand was already thinning out when we went back to look for the Lords. Hollis had put on a pair of glasses and was examining a newspaper folded on his knee, his eyes half lidded as he tapped a pencil against his chin. It was one of those rare moments when you could see the melancholy lines in his face. Lida stood beside him, as still as a statue, gazing sightlessly at the horizon. They looked so lonely amid a half acre of empty chairs.

"We're back," Erin called to them.

They turned to us, startled. "Ah! You've decided to stay a while longer," Hollis said, his face filling with pleasure. His pencil and the forgotten crossword puzzle slid from his knee as he stood, putting an arm around Erin. "Wonderful!"

"After all, we can go back tomorrow," I said. "Right?"

"Right," said Lida, her eyes shining. She squeezed my hand and kissed me on the mouth. "I'm starved," she confided to me. "What about you?"

6

BACK IN OUR hotel room Erin and I washed up, tussled on the bed half clothed, got dressed and walked down the hall and around to the Lords' room. The Lords' quarters were much more spacious and more elegantly furnished than ours — they had a pair of dark mahogany bureaus, an oval marble-topped table and they even had a fireplace with a marble mantel and above it a large mirror in a heavy gilt frame. Furthermore, their place had a nice folding screen with pink satin panels to stand in front of the doorway that connected our rooms. Lida wanted Erin to take a pullover with her, in case the restaurant was air conditioned or the evening turned chill. She had opened a suitcase on the bed and now she tumbled the clothing about and came up with three light sweaters. They were a bit big for Erin, but to be polite she took one and that seemed to please Lida.

We had a wonderful time that evening. It turned out that the first restaurant Hollis drove to had a long line of irritable patrons waiting to be seated, and so did the second, but the third place was a small tavern that Erin spotted at the bottom of a side street. Up front there was a bar with a few unpainted tables and chairs, and when you walked through the kitchen and stepped out back you found a grape arbor with Japanese lanterns strung about and maybe a dozen tables with white table cloths and little bowls with citronella candles to keep off the mosquitoes. It wasn't a finicky place. At the end of the arbor the owners had nailed together a lattice fence through which you could see the tavern's trash barrels and cars passing on the next street, and from time to time you could hear a shout or a car door slam or a dog barking. There was one empty table. "This is fine! Let's sit down and order," Hollis said, drawing out a chair for Lida.

"Or we may soon begin to eat each other," said Lida, smiling in a way to show her teeth.

"And which one of us would you choose to eat?" Hollis asked soberly, putting on his glasses and tilting back his head to read the menu on his plate. But Erin told her not to answer. "You'll hurt somebody's feelings when they get left out," Erin said. The cook couldn't have produced a fancy dish if he had tried, but we didn't want fancy dishes. The food was good, the wine was good and the conversation went all over the lot. We enjoyed ourselves immensely. Long after we had finished dinner we sat there drinking wine and talking, talking about Eisenhower, British cars, upstate Chablis, the Red Sox, sculpture, French films, horse racing and on and on. Little by little the brightness had faded from the sky and now it was black and we could see lights winking through the lattice fence whenever a car drove by. Hollis and Lida were sitting across from Erin and me, the same as in the restaurant by the train station, but here it was dark all around us and their faces were illuminated by the candles on our table. It was hard to believe that we had met them only twenty-four hours ago. The Lords were radiant that evening and seemed to reflect back to us the heat and excitement Erin and I felt around each other. In fact, since meeting Erin the world had filled with prodigal generosity and the Lords were part of it. Their eyes sparkled, their faces glowed, and looking at them I felt we all knew each other better and liked each other much more than people who had been together for only a day.

I had never really noticed it before: Hollis and Lida were a good looking couple. Hollis, of course, had the lean features and hardy slenderness of a man who had run cross-country in college. Lida was wearing a sleeve-less dress with mere strings for straps, and it revealed the shoulders and arms of a powerful swimmer. "No, not from swimming," she told me. "Just from hammer-ing away at my blocks of wood. And stone, when I can afford it." Looking at them side by side now, this hand-some couple, this pair of well-matched athletes, I saw them for the first time also as husband and wife, as part-ners, and I wondered — just for a moment here and a moment there — how they regarded each other, what they did when they were alone together, how they made love. Lida had interesting features: thick brown hair with lighter streaks of yellowish brown and glints of black, large hazel eyes, and those wide Slavic cheekbones. I wasn't drawn to her but I saw how any man might be. She made you aware of her solid presence. Her fingers were strong, the nails trimmed close, and as we talked she would occasionally arch her back and rub her hand slowly across the nape of her neck, or she would idly clasp her bare shoulder or stroke her smooth round arm in a slow forgetful fashion. Now and again when she spoke about Hollis she put her hand on his shoulder, and once while I was talking she reached across the table and gently closed her hand on my wrist, meaning to interrupt me to ask a question. Maybe I should not have been so surprised when she kissed me at the race track this afternoon. The surprise had blotted over any other feeling, and it was only as we sat talking in the candle light that I began to recover the abrupt touch of her mouth, a lingering instant, then the quick sweep of her eyes into me as she withdrew.

I watched her now as she began to light a cigarette, looked at her lips and speculated how it felt to Hollis when he kissed her mouth, or what that mouth felt like to him on his flesh, here or there or anywhere. Lida glanced across at me, then abruptly waved out the match and crushed the cigarette into the ashtray. "What say we go around to a coffee house and sober up? All this wine has made me light headed," she announced. Hollis drained his glass and asked Erin and me what we thought of going. We said it sounded fine to us. Hollis and I split the bill. Instead of threading our way back through the kitchen and bar and out the front door we simply walked around the lattice fence to the next street.

Hollis and Erin were walking side by side, a few steps ahead of Lida and me. He tilted his head to Erin and said something, but we couldn't quite catch it. Erin began to laugh.

"Alcohol goes straight to my head," Lida told me.

"Then I do foolish things. I've had too much, do you think?"

"No. You look fine to me."

"Wait!" She halted, kneeling to adjust her sandal. "Just a minute." She began to unlace the thongs that wound about her ankle. She straightened up with the sandal in hand, turning away from me to examine it in the light of the street lamp. "So, so, so, so. Well. It's not broken, Bart. —How do you suppose it did that?"

"Did what? What's wrong?"

But she had already knelt again on the sidewalk and now began to retie the thongs. "It wasn't broken. It just came undone," she explained, working on it. Erin and Hollis turned the corner at the end of the block and disappeared from view. A moment later Lida stood up and kissed me on the mouth, her hands resting lightly on my shoulders, and when my hands went to her hips she stepped forward, closing her arms, her hands rising along the back of my neck, her fingers in my hair. She withdrew with that quiet, rippling laugh of hers. "What do you think those two are doing around the corner?" she asked.

I still breathed the scent of her perfume and tobacco, still felt her flesh opening on mine. "Nothing dramatic, I hope."

"God forbid," said Lida. "Let's not get heavy and dramatic."

"Listen, this is —" I broke off, confused.

"What? This is what?" she prompted.

I laughed. "Not serious."

She smiled. "We do like you so much. This isn't meant to be dramatic, either. We just like you, both of you. And we're serious about that."

"We feel the same about you," I said. "Both of you."

"When we get around this corner we may catch them in the middle of something exciting. What do you think?"

"I think we're too late," I said. We had turned the corner just after Hollis had shut the passenger door and was walking around to the driver's side. The driver's door opened — we could see Erin as she leaned across to unlatch it — and now Hollis ducked in and pulled the door shut behind him. We walked down the sidewalk to the car. "Maybe we'll have better luck next time," Lida said in a conspiratorial whisper, her lips close to my ear.

The coffee house was packed. It was all one room: a busy espresso bar at the near end and a low platform at the other and a score of tables crammed in between, each one no bigger than a dinner plate. Hollis and Lida managed to edge their way down to a table on that wall, and we pressed ourselves sideways along this wall to a table a bit further back. A young woman with long flat blond hair had appeared on the shallow stage and now she seated herself on the solitary stool and began to tune her guitar. The crowd gradually ceased talking. The young woman played her guitar and sang folk songs, some ballads of sly humor but mostly sad songs of love and loss, rivalry, vengeance and death. The room was quiet, save for the occasional hiss of the espresso machine, the plink of a spoon or the click of a cup being set in its saucer. We could see the Lords on the other side of the room, leaning their heads together (now this way, now that) as if in whispered conversation. When the singer had completed her set, they appeared at our table.

"We're going back to the hotel, but we're leaving the car with you," Hollis said, cheerfully. "Don't want to cut short your evening." He lifted his hand to forestall my saying anything.

"We're taking a cab," Lida added. "More exciting."

"Hey, wait —" I began.

"Keys," Hollis said. "This one's the ignition. Glove compartment, trunk."

"We can't —" Erin start to speak.

They said I should drive the Jaguar just as I drove the VW, but with more dignity, said we should have a good time. After they left, Erin and I ordered a second cup of coffee.

"That was decent of them," I said.

"Yes."

I wondered how to tell Erin about Lida without giving it more meaning than it deserved.

"Hollis was forward this evening," Erin remarked.

"What do you mean, *forward*?"

"I mean we were walking along, laughing about something and he put his arm around my shoulders and when I turned to look at him he kissed me."

"Oh?" I was surprised and yet not surprised at the same time, if such a state is possible. "Well. Now I know what you mean by forward."

"I'm sorry I brought it up. He didn't mean anything by it."

"I understand, I understand." I put on a thoughtful frown and tried to compose myself.

"You do understand?"

"Yes. Lida's the same way."

"Lida? You mean —" She broke off and started to laugh. "What do you mean?"

During the next set of folk songs we squeezed up from the table and inched our way along the wall to the door. It was cool outside. Erin put on the sweater she had borrowed, a large white loosely knit garment which she said cost a fortune. "I feel like a ball of twine. How do I look?" she asked. She looked great and I told her so. She had lifted a fistful of sweater from between her breasts and was holding it to her nose. "Lida's perfume. Spicy. I'll have to ask her what it is." It was nice to drive Hollis's Jaguar, trim but cushy compared to the VW. Outside the town I stepped on the gas and put the car through its paces, scooting over a couple of hillocks and around the curves leading to the hotel. When we got to our room I put the car keys on the bureau along with the other stuff from my pockets, so I'd find them in the morning. Then we took a shower together and lay on the bed in our towels, Erin on her back and me on my side, propped on my elbow, looking at her. Her body seemed to have gathered to itself all the light in the room and her flesh glowed, just as a pond or a tranquil river does right after the sun has set.

I don't know how long we stayed that way. Erin had put her hand in my hair, just the tips of her fingers combing it back gently, tenderly, all the while watching my eyes while I looked at her. Then there must have been a soft ripple across the silence, a sound or glimmer at the other end of the room. We glanced at the closed door that led to the Lords' suite. I got up and went over to it, saw that the bolt was shut. A narrow wedge of light ran between the door and the jamb — the old place had settled out of plumb long ago — and clearly the door on the other side was open. Erin had come up beside me. I pressed one hand flat against the latch side of our door and cautiously turned the knob, hoping to close it more snugly. It didn't budge. Erin knelt impulsively and peered through the keyhole. I put my eye to the open wedge of light and felt her hand clamp on my thigh. The door on the other side was drifting very slowly open and we could spy, as if just beyond reach, the folding screen with its pink satin panels transmuted to dark rose in the near shadow. Beyond the edge of the screen we could see across the room to the fireplace where Hollis stood in profile in an effeminate violet dressing gown, one hand on the marble mantel, observing Lida who now knelt to face him in an old fashioned corset. The sides of the corset were so deeply hollowed and the laces so cruelly tight that it became a narrow-waisted vase, her gleaming shoulders and breasts and upturned face all part of an exquisite bouquet held out to him, her buttocks flaring beneath, large and white — all this in the dusky rose ambience of the antique table lamp and its reflection in the gilded mirror. His face, dark and concentrated, seemed about to drive down upon her, and he trembled as if he were holding himself back only by the greatest will. The ring on his finger grated abruptly on the marble and a moving gleam made visible the slender chain that ran from his hand to the high Victorian choker Lida wore around her neck. She continued to look steadfastly into his eyes and now tucked her arms into the small of her back. The folds of his dressing gown parted with a rustle and silken hiss.

I jerked back and looked at Erin, her eye at the keyhole while her nails bit slowly into my thigh. I pulled her hand from my leg and she turned to glare at me, her mouth half open and her cheeks as red as if she had been slapped. I dropped down, dragging her to the floor, but she had already torn the towel from my waist and now grabbed at me, seized my stiffening flesh, let go as if scorched, grabbed again and began pumping in furious silence while we rolled noiselessly this way and that on the rug. The sweat made our bodies slick and when I tried to drag her to the bed she slipped from me, then sank down under and pulled me in, so we coupled there on the rug, our mouths open in wordless cries. Some minutes later we crept back to peer through the slit to the Lords' room. Lida was standing by the fireplace in her laced corset and black stockings, half turned toward us. She had removed the glittering choker from her neck and was trying to disentangle it from the chain, a small knot of concentration between her brows. Hollis's torso passed close in front of us, blotting out the view — one more moment of rosy lamp light and the door came quietly shut.

7

THE NEXT MORNING I slipped out of bed while Erin was still sleeping. I didn't know how I felt about Hollis and Lida, and I didn't know what to think about Erin and me and the way we had gone at each other last night. We had made love again and again until there was only a raw itch and then had fallen into an exhausted sleep. I pulled up the shade and looked at the green fields and distant green hills, and tried to lose myself out there. Erin stirred behind me and I turned to see her roll over and slide languidly head first from the bed — her hand struck the floor and her black mane of hair slid forward from the nape of her neck and unfurled over her dangling arm. She lifted her head, looked at me a moment, then let her head fall back again. She remained that way, silent and not moving. I knew she was thinking about last night and I was afraid she was convinced she had made a big mistake, several big mistakes, and now she would want to get as far away from me as she could. "Are we still friends?" she asked, not looking up. I told her I certainly hoped so. She pushed herself up, sat on the edge of the bed and pulled the sheet across her lap. She had never hidden herself that way before. "We're animals," she said flatly.

"That, too," I said. I had the mournful thought that she would pull the sheet over her breasts and ask me to toss her some clothes.

She flung the sheet aside and headed to the bathroom, throwing her arms about and saying, "Dogs? Pigs? What kind of animal? Horses? I'd prefer to think horses."

She slammed the bathroom door behind her.

Later, while I was shaving, she told me that we were supposed to meet the Lords between 10:30 and 11:00 in their room. "We're going out for brunch. Remember?" No, I didn't remember. "We arranged it last night over dinner." Yes, I remembered vaguely. Erin came and stood in the doorway, leaning against the doorjamb. How come I didn't use an electric razor, she wanted to know. I told her I didn't like noise early in the morning. Had I ever shaved my pubic hair, she asked. "God, no!" I said. She shrugged. I needn't sound so shocked. Women have to shave *their* pubic hair — at least at the margins — or it shows around the edge of the swim suit, she informed me. I said I hadn't thought about that. Had I thought about the Lords, she wanted to know. I had thought about them, yes.

"What's going on?" she asked.

"I don't know," I said.

So we talked about Hollis and Lida and especially about what we had seen behind the door last night. Erin asked me what I thought of the way the Lords went about making love. I said I didn't know what to think of it, but I did like Hollis and Lida and was ashamed to think badly of them. "I suppose every couple has its own way of making love, its own style," I ventured.

Erin smiled. "Yeah. Well. That looked to me like a rather somewhat elaborate style."

"How many people have you looked at making love? How can you make comparisons?"

"Now be reasonable. How many people do you think lead up to it that way?"

"I don't know. Maybe Hollis and Lida are more theatrical than most people."

"Well, I didn't like the play they were acting in," she said with finality.

I started to smile and turned to look at her. "Come

on, Erin. You were excited by it."

"Only because I never saw anyone making love before. *That* excited me — the sight of people fucking. Don't laugh!"

"But we didn't actually see that part. We saw —"

"All right all right all right," she broke in. "I admit I got excited. Of course I got excited. Because I knew what was coming. I knew what they were going to do later. That's all."

I didn't say anything. I rinsed out my razor and shaving brush while Erin stayed there, leaning against the bathroom doorjamb with her arms folded, watching me and waiting. "What?" I asked her, drying my face.

"You mean to say you were aroused by that little Victorian drama of master and, and, and — That debauched version of Jane Eyre or something? Is that what excited you?" she asked.

I escaped past her and pulled on my shirt. "I don't know exactly. We saw so many things all at once — the tight corset, the bare flesh, the way she knelt down. Even the way we were watching them aroused —"

"Don't forget the chain," she cut in sharply.

"I haven't forgotten the chain."

"The chain was a big part of it. That and the look on his face," she added.

I had begun to feel shy and embarrassed talking about the scene and especially uncomfortable talking about Hollis, had begun to feel as if I were betraying him. I busied myself with buttoning my cuffs, so I wouldn't have to face Erin. "I thought the look on his face was natural enough. He was about to take her. It was the look on *her* face that shocked me," I said.

"I didn't see anything shocking in her face," Erin said vaguely.

"When Lida looked up at him she had a look of complicity. That did it for me. It was her look that made the whole scene, made it —" I hesitated, searching for the word.

Erin had taken up her comb and now turned to the mirror. "I guess I was watching him, mostly. Watching her was too humiliating." She pulled the comb through her hair in long even strokes without speaking for a while. "I don't know why I'm so critical of them. I still like them. And God knows we were swept away last night. They put on a good performance," she added.

"How did we get to be drama critics?"

"Maybe that whole scene was staged for us," Erin said, laying down her comb.

I had been wondering about that, too. We debated what had drawn us to the door, whether it had been a small noise or a glimmer of light. We agreed that when we peered through we had seen the Lords' door moving ever so slightly by itself. Maybe it had not been bolted properly, or maybe they had unlocked it when they thought they were locking it, or maybe they had simply given it an extra push shut, just to be secure, and that push had caused it to unlatch and bounce a bit and swing open behind their backs. Anyway, the door frame had fallen out of plumb long ago and the door hung crookedly now, so it would swing open if left unlatched. We figured that Hollis and Lida would not have purposely undone the latch and made a noise to draw us to the door. Or even if they had, they could not have counted on our watching them. At least, they could not have expected us to get caught up and set on fire the way we had. We were sure of that.

We walked down the hall and around to the Lords' room. I had expected it would be awkward to meet their eyes, but of course they didn't know that we had spied on them last night and they were friendly and open and obviously happy to see us, asking questions about the coffee house and how long had we stayed there and had we liked the singer and had the Jaguar behaved all right. I gave Hollis the keys and thanked him and said it had been a treat to drive, and he began to tell me about a sports car rally which was held, or used to be held, in a nearby town. The violet dressing robe hung negligently at the end of the folding screen, tossed there and forgotten. We stood in the middle of the room in idle conversation, and I could feel everything in my head shift around and around and around. A short while earlier Erin and I had been superior and critical of the Lords' sexual style and had indulged ourselves in trying to figure out if they had staged their bedroom scene with us in mind. We had talked about them as if they were deceptive frauds. But now I was beginning to feel uneasy about ourselves. Erin had given back the sweater she had borrowed last night and was asking Lida something about perfume, and now she held Lida close, as if to kiss her cheek or ear, drinking the spicy scent while the older woman threw her head back and laughed. Erin held onto Lida and I guessed she felt the same as I, felt that we were the low frauds. Then Hollis gave me a friendly pat on the back and we went out.

Hollis drove us to the Gideon Putnam, a swank hotel in the woods a short way outside of town. Just as we were walking in he began to tell us who Gideon Putnam was, but Lida looked at him with a weary smile and he broke off with a jest. The new place was made of brick and along the front stood white pillars that went up three stories to an overhanging roof, an architectural memory of the style the old Saratoga hotels had favored — that was something I had learned from Hollis, of course. There was a fair crowd in the dining hall, but the room was spacious and light. It turned out we all were very, very hungry: apparently we had worked up an appetite last night. We were seated beside one of the tall windows that overlooked the grounds and we agreed it would be pleasant to go for a stroll after brunch, but instead we lingered over our coffee, talking of one thing and another.

Erin induced Lida to speak about her sculptures. At first she was reluctant to say much, so Hollis would tell us about a piece he liked or he would inform us about her technique or begin a lecture on theory, and Lida would break in to explain this or that point and in a little while she was talking freely about her work. She had tried her hand at drawing and painting, and according to Hollis she was a good draftsman, but she had always come back to sculpture. "You can walk around it and you can touch it — it's not an illusion," she said. She had worked in clay and in stone and even in cloth, in sheet metal, plastic, cast bronze and cast iron, but for the past several years she had been working with wood, nothing but wood, only wood.

"I touch metal or stone and it's always hotter or colder than I am. But wood is friendly to touch. We have the same temperature." She smiled and put the back of her hand lightly against Erin's cheek, as if to sense her temperature, but instead she brushed the cheek with a caress. Then she turned to me and said, "Lucky man," and glanced straight into my eyes for an instant.

Erin laughed and tossed her head in a quick, pleasurable shudder, causing her long black hair to shake nervously.

Lida explained that wood was alive, that it breathed, that it lived when it was a tree and was still alive after it had been chopped down and sawed into blocks. I had never thought about the cell structure of wood or about any of the other things she went on to talk about and I was intrigued by what she was saying. But, as a matter of fact, the longer I watched her talking the more I was distracted — distracted by the way she had stroked Erin's cheek, by her manner of showing us her open palm to illustrate something, by the luxurious fashion in which she stretched her arm and massaged the hollow of her elbow. And the longer she spoke, the more pronounced her accent grew, certain words coming from her tongue with such a warm rough texture that I paid no attention to their meaning and lost track of what she was saying. I let myself think about her kneeling in the lamplight of the hotel bedroom, in the satin bondage of that corset, the chain glittering on her collar — I felt her mouth opening obediently under mine, caught the scent of her perfume — abruptly came to my senses at the table.

"Because each block of wood has its own character," Lida was saying. "It's in the grain. I shape it and the wood responds and I can feel it respond. I like that."

Erin asked if she wasn't afraid the wood might split when it dried out. She mentioned a tall, post-like piece she had seen at Lida's East Side exhibit: that piece had some small open cracks in it.

Lida said she knew the piece Erin referred to and, yes, it was cracking, checking. "It's aging. It's still alive and getting older. And it's drying out, like me, like this piece," she added, dropping her hand to her thigh with a slap. She laughed.

Hollis said it was time to go out for a stroll before we aged any more. The hotel was located at the edge of what appeared to be an endless park, a patchwork of pine groves and green fields and, according to the Lords, there were mineral springs scattered throughout. While Hollis and I were deciding which way to go, Lida and Erin drifted down a gravel path toward a grove of trees, so we followed. Our path went through a colonnade of pines, where we met an oncoming troop of people in white suits and long white dresses, and then came out onto another green acre of nicely mowed grass. A small party of men and women were unpacking a box of mallets and setting wickets into the lawn. They waved and called out, asking if we wanted to join them for a game of croquet, but we called back no and thank you and waved goodbye. I had already taken off my jacket, had pulled off my necktie and unbuttoned my shirt, but it still felt hot as we crossed the open green. There was an older couple way ahead of us, the woman carrying a parasol, and Lida remarked that parasols were certainly not stylish but she wished she had one now. We were approaching a low reddish building — "Swimming pool," Lida said — with people picnicking nearby.

When we finally reached the building and climbed the shallow steps we saw that it was indeed a swimming pool. It was a long squared-off brick structure with changing rooms on the four sides and a long rectangular pool in the middle — as if a child had tried to build a Pompeian villa with blocks. The four of us leaned on a balustrade where we could survey the pool and the scores of swimmers plowing in every direction, thrashing about and kicking up a great spray. We were about six feet above the pool terrace and sometimes we got sprinkled by the flying water. We agreed that swimming was a grand idea, but that the pool was over-crowded and we weren't sorry that we had no swimsuits with us. After a while Erin and Lida were ready to continue our walk, but Hollis and I tarried at the rail to look over the swimmers and the people sunbathing all around the margin of the pool. We were watching a young woman in the water close beneath us when suddenly she surged upward, grabbed the edge of the pool and pulled herself onto the terrace, letting the water sluice down her breasts and buttocks and legs and rain around her. She had a neat compact torso and long legs and while she was toweling her arms she glanced up and smiled at us. Hollis and I waved back. Lida announced that Hollis and I were getting a lot more out of this spectator sport than she and Erin were. Erin agreed. Lida asked did she want to go to a spa bath house. "This may seem like a dumb question," Erin said. "But what exactly do you do in a bath house?"

"We get a bath and a luxurious massage. How does that sound?"

"Sounds great to me," Erin said.

8

AFTER LIDA and Erin left, Hollis and I turned back to lean our elbows on the balustrade and resume our survey of the swimmers and sunbathers. The young woman who had smiled up at us had given her towel to a muscular friend who was grinning and talking to her while he dried his broad hairless chest and arms. When he finished with the towel, they spread it on the concrete margin and sat down on it. It was pleasant to stand here in the cool of the arcade and to watch the endless diving and shuttling of the swimmers. The sunlight bounced up from the sky-blue basin of the pool and danced in the air, mingling with the shrieks of children, the shouting of the older kids and the calls of mothers and fathers. Swimming pools are happy places.

"It's as close as we can get to flying," Hollis said, breaking in on my reverie. "When we're swimming in a clear pool of water we feel weightless. We can swoop down or up, we can dart here or there — it's like flying, like being an angel."

"Maybe that's part of it," I said. "But these swimmers are obviously delighting in their bodies. Angels can't do that. Angels have no bodies."

"No bodies? Certainly angels have bodies."

"Not in the usual sense, no. Angels are spirits created by God, having understanding and free will. — It goes something like that. I used to know it by heart from my catechism. Angels don't have bodies, don't have parents, don't have children," I added.

"No bodies," he said reflectively, dubious.

We discussed the nature of angels and how it is that we can see them and portray them, even though they have no bodies, and Hollis remarked that being weightless would be a great advantage in making love, but being bodiless would ruin it. "Well, you can't be an angel and make love at the same time," I said. Hollis laughed. It was one of my uncles who told me that, I confessed. He asked was my uncle a theologian. I said no, he had been called many names, but theologian wasn't among them. I began to tell Hollis about some of my uncles and aunts, but he offered nothing about his own family and instead he returned to an earlier point in our conversation. For if angels have understanding but don't have a body, he wondered what it was they understood. "Everything I truly understand, I understand because I have a body," he said. "What can a bodiless angel understand?"

I thought about it a minute and suggested mathematics. Hollis said I made mathematics sound like desolation, and he asked was I unhappy with it. I told him I was, that I was unhappy with it precisely because it was bodiless. At one time that didn't matter to me, but now it did. "I don't know what I want. Not mathematics. Not quantum mechanics. I don't know what I want," I told him.

Hollis looked thoughtfully at the swimmers, the sunbathers and the kids running about. "Well, as for me —" he said. He trailed off, for we had begun to watch a woman in a glistening black swimsuit who had mounted the ladder to the diving platform and stood there holding onto the guard rails, her body straight, her face a meditative mask. Now she stalked to the end of the board and sprang up, her body elongating and — as if her hands had reached to an invisible trapeze — her legs in rigid parallel swung up and over till she stood upside down in the air, paused, then plunged from the sky to slit the water with barely a splash. "I always wanted to be a painter," Hollis said, watching the diver — her body moving in slow, distorted ripples as she swam under water to the far end of the pool.

"A painter?" I said, surprised.

He turned to me with half a smile. "That shocks you? Did you think I grew up wanting to run a small gallery of eighteenth and nineteenth century Americana in eastern Massachusetts? Yes, a painter."

"Oh. It's just that —" I broke off, sorry that I had blundered and hurt his feelings.

"What?"

"You talk so well— You know so much— You're so intellectual that I assumed—"

"Yes. Well. I wasn't always like this. As a matter of fact, as a kid I was quite dumb. I didn't have a way of thinking about things and I didn't have a talent for talk. I wasn't good company and I liked being alone. Or, to be truthful, I was left by myself a lot. I was left alone. I grew up being a spectator and I spent a lot of time with a sketch pad. Drawing was a solace. I liked to look at things and I liked to draw, but as luck would have it I wasn't a particularly good draftsman. I know now that being a skilled draftsman doesn't matter. I mean, you can be an artist, even a great artist, and still not be a particularly good draftsman. Those people at country fairs who can draw you a likeness in two minutes or cut a true silhouette while you sit there — they're handy with a pencil but they're not artists. It's the vision that makes all the difference. You have a vision and you put it on canvas, no matter what. —I don't know why I'm boring you with all this," he said abruptly.

"You're not boring me at all," I protested.

He looked at me a moment, as if to test the truth of what I said, then slapped my shoulder and laughed. "You're good company. Have I told you how much I like you? Well, I do. Anyway, I went into art history. I took one or two studio courses, but mostly I sat in a library and read books or I sat in a darkened lecture hall and looked at pictures projected on a screen." He turned back to the pool. "Where did she go?" he asked.

He meant the diver in the black swimsuit. We found she had climbed from the pool at the far end and was standing there — one hand automatically jerked the hem of her swimsuit down over her haunch — talking with a couple of men and women. One of the women was holding a baby on her hip and now the diver gave the baby a kiss.

"So, by the time I left college I was an intellectual," Hollis said, gazing passively at the diver as she walked along the far edge of the pool. "At least, that's what I thought of myself. I was so marvelously intellectual that the notion of looking at something and putting a vision of it on canvas struck me as a kind of mindless talent, something on the level of an automatic reflex — like blinking when you get a speck in your eye. On the other hand, what the art critic did was important and required brains and effort. The artist was inarticulate — that's why he painted — and his work of art was dumb. That's where the critic came in. The work of art was like a beautiful musical instrument and the critic was the only one who could play it, who could give it a voice, who could pick it up and perform with it like a virtuoso. And, after all, it's the performance that counts, not the dumb instrument." He laughed, mocking himself.

I was interested in whatever Hollis was willing to tell me about himself, but listening to him was like becoming familiar with the ins and outs of a thesis and not at all like getting to know someone. I asked what his mother and father had thought of his drawings when he was a kid, and he shrugged and said, "They thought it was a nice hobby," and then resumed the analysis of his career. And later when I asked if he had any brothers or sisters, he said, "One brother and one sister and they both have children. And what do you say to getting some of the local water at one of the pavilions when we leave here?" so I didn't ask him anything else about his family, and I didn't talk about my uncles or my grandfather Cavallù.

"That woman on the diving board fascinates me," Hollis said. "I enjoy watching her. I have absolutely nothing to say about her. If I could, I would get it all on canvas — that body in all this light and water. But no words, none. I enjoy the sight and I have no desire to add words to it. No theories about the body. No interpretations of it. Just the thing itself. I want to go back to being dumb again."

I smiled. "You can't do that. It's too late now to go back."

He laughed amiably. "I know, I know. It happened in Eden. It's called the Fall of Man. It's in your catechism somewhere."

The woman in the shimmering black swimsuit stood at the top of the ladder with her hands gripping the silvery guard rails, her head down as if she were studying her flat stomach.

"Do we stay to watch, or do we go for that water?" I

asked him. The diver lifted her chin and raised herself on her toes, the muscle rising along her legs, glistening.

"Actually, she doesn't fascinate me but the image does," he said, squinting up at her. "I would like to speak those images without words, images of the body, the actual body — not the angelic incorporeal body — but our body, yours and mine and hers, the mortal body. There's a language there. I'm sure of it. There's a language in our bodies, but I don't know how to speak it."

What he said seemed to echo something Erin had said to me the night before last, and just then I might have told him so, but he had already turned to leave the pool. At the crest of her flight, the woman rolled onto her back, her sleek body tense and exultant now as she stretched upon her high bed of air, arching her back and lifting her pelvis upward even as she sailed over and began to come down. We heard the water plunge and surge behinds us, then we turned the corner and descended the shallow steps to the grass.

We went to a small pavilion made of yellow-and-white stripped canvas, like one of those tents put up at fairs, where they sold ice cream and soft drinks and small bottles of what Hollis called "the local water." We both bought a bottle and sat on a bench in the shade at the edge of a grove of pines. The bottles had a nice old-fashioned label with curlicues, but the water didn't taste much different from plain carbonated water. I had long since unbuttoned my shirt and rolled up my sleeves and now Hollis, too, pulled off his necktie and began to unbutton his shirt. We began talking about bodies again, about images of the body without words. Actually, it was Hollis who did most of the talking while I drank the local seltzer and listened. As he talked he reached inside his freshly opened shirt and scratched and rubbed his chest, idly chaffing the hair. The memory of his body came back from last night, the robe half open and his chest hair burning in the glow of the lamp. But when the robe had completely opened, had parted with a silken sigh, I had turned away. From the time we had first seen the Lords in their room this morning until this moment now — watching him run his hand slowly inside his collar to loosen it a bit more, watching him push his fingers through his chest hair — I had not thought about his embracing Erin, kissing Erin. I thought about it now, thought about him with his arm around her shoulders, kissing her, and my hand leapt out and knocked his hand aside. "What the hell —" he began.

"A bee. Just a bee. Don't worry. It's gone now," I explained. I supposed it was natural for him to want to do that with Erin, but I felt sorry for him if he thought it was going to go anywhere, because I knew it wasn't — and, in fact, I felt a little ashamed about knowing as much about it as I knew.

"But you two are in love," he said.

"What?"

"I said, you two are in love. And you've know each other for a year or so. Right?"

"Yes," I said.

"Which makes it impossible for you to think in terms of pure body, of the flesh and so on."

I had lost the thread of the conversation and must have looked puzzled.

Hollis smiled. "All I mean is, when you look at Erin you don't see, you can't see, her body as the beautiful creation it is. You're in love with her and —"

"Why should that stop me from —" I began to say.

"And when you look at her, when you look at her unclothed, especially when you look at her while making love you see much more than a body. You see a kingdom, perhaps, a realm, a future world, a — "

"Everything," I said.

"Exactly," he said. "Everything."

We began a meandering walk across those endless lawns to the spa bath house, hoping to arrive there around the time what Erin and Lida would be coming out. That section of the park was absolutely level and the grass was mowed so short that it looked like a putting green. There weren't many people about. The lonely spa buildings were one-storey oblongs made of brick, mostly, but outlined with some other material — maybe limestone, maybe stucco or concrete — and each one had large multi-paned windows of opaque glass along the sides, and there were pillars and empty statuary niches in the front. Some of the structures were arranged in a neat symmetrical pattern about a large rectangular reflecting pool, and there were walkways or colonnades — I don't know the precise term — that went part of the way from one building to the next, but then stopped. I asked Hollis who had built this strange place, and he told me New York State did it. There were stone lintels or entablatures laid atop the columns, making big empty doorways, and these entablatures had mottos or poetry or something carved into them. We had been talking about the Red Sox, debating whether Yastrzemski was going to be as great a player as Williams, but we began to read the sayings and they were so strange that I copied some down. One said:

WITH POTENT MINERAL
SALTS IMBUED THIS CUP
HAS VIRTUES MEDICINAL FOR
FRAIL AND MORTAL MAN

And another one:

THESE VALES WITH SPRINGS
IMBOSOMED IN THEIR WOODS

We were reading these odd things when we heard our names being called from a distance and turned to see Erin and Lida coming down the steps from one of the buildings. They waved to us and they both looked very happy. "Erin likes Lida very much," I said.

"And Lida took a quick liking to your Erin. We both did. Sometimes I think Lida comes on too strong, too fast. I'm used to it, but she has a passion that frightens some people."

"She's fine. I like Lida."

"That's good. She's attracted to you. Strongly. I hope you don't mind."

Then they were here and there wasn't any time to think about what he had said.

9

THAT AFTERNOON Erin and I stayed in Saratoga while the Lords drove off to Lake George to look at an art exhibit. A gallery up there was showing the work of Alfred Stieglitz and Georgia O'Keeffe who used to spend their summers together in a big house on the shore of the lake. The trip was Lida's idea. She explained that she wasn't fascinated by O'Keeffe paintings, but she admired the woman and wanted to take the drive. They invited us along but we begged off and, in fact, I think they were happy to be without us for a while. We walked down to the hotel driveway with them to say goodbye. "Don't hold dinner. Don't know what hour we'll be back," Lida called out, waving from the car window. The Jaguar glided away. We went up to our room, tore off our clothes and fell on each other. I hadn't even thought about making love but when we got into the room everything came rushing in a frenzy, as if we had been denying ourselves for a week.

Afterward we lay on our backs on the bed to catch our breath, both of us slick with sweat, our hands and ankles just touching. I felt it had happened too fast. A soft breeze filled the curtains and tipped them slowly into the room, holding them there like bells or pale flowers before they rippled and fluttered back down to the window. Erin murmured that it wasn't a bad life, being a cloud, just drifting, coming up here, dissolving there. That's the way she felt just now and, come to think of it, that's the way she had felt after the massage, she said. We floated in the sweet quiet for a while. I asked her if the spa bath was really different from any other bath.

"Well, the water smells a little rotten," she answered languorously.

"I thought you said you liked it."

"I did like it. But it does smell a little rotten. It feels nice. It's carbonated and when it comes up from the spring all these tiny bubbles get free and run wild in it, so it's like taking a bath in seltzer water."

I asked if she could actually feel the bubbles.

"All over, everywhere," she said, getting up and going to the bureau. "I've decided to give up cigarettes, but I want one now." Erin lit a cigarette, then settled into the baggy wicker chair by the window, drew up her legs and placed the ashtray on the window sill. She began to talk idly about the spa pavilion and the baths.

The entrance way to the baths was a large noisy, echoing room with bare walls and a polished stone floor. The concierge, of whatever you call her, was seated in a glass booth in the middle of the place, a busy and rather distracted woman much like a ticket seller in the lobby of a movie house. On the counter inside her booth she had spread out half a dozen notebooks, charts and cards, and was constantly shifting them about, as if she were playing a complicated game of solitaire. She told them the fee for a bath and massage, took their money and directed them through a large doorway at the side, and moved two cards from one side of the counter to the top of a notebook. The doorway led into a wide corridor with tile walls and oak benches along the sides, and one of the women attendants was pushing a wagon stacked with towels. For a moment Erin felt as if they were trooping down the hall that led from the locker room to the gymnasium at college, but here the attendants wore the loose white uniforms of a hospital clinic. Erin and Lida were given neighboring rooms, each bare white cell furnished with a high-walled tub and a bed, plus an alcove and john. One of the attendants, a little old lady, turned on the water and chatted about the fine weather and left when the tub was filled. The water was hot but not scalding. Erin slipped out of her clothes, stepped warily into the tub and then cautiously lay back until her head rested on the rim and the water just barely licked her chin. "It was new to me to lie half-floating in a deep tub of water for no reason except to feel good. I tried to think what we had said the other night when we were talking about bodies and what they mean, but I couldn't remember and after a while I had to stop trying. Because there I was floating in this warm carbonated water with all these bubbles swirling over my flesh and flooding my head and turning every thought to liquid."

I told her about a psychological theory which claims we like to float in baths because it brings back subconscious memories of our aqueous life in the womb.

In response, Erin merely lolled her head way back on the old wicker chair and watched the smoke she let drift from her half open mouth. A while later she said, "I loved it even better when the little attendant came back and wrapped me in a hot sheet. That was delicious."

"That was the best part?"

"The massage was the best part." Erin snubbed out her cigarette, then came back to the bed and lay down on her side, facing me. She put her hand on my chest and brushed her fingers against the nap of hair. "Massage is what we long for. Massage is the way to my heart. Massage is better than anything — except you, of course," she told me.

"I'm honored. How long does the massage go on?"

"Half an hour."

"We can go on longer than that," I said. "That last one was too brief."

"At least, it was supposed to go on for half an hour. Actually, Lida came in before the masseuse had finished with me and they got to talking about Swedish massage and Japanese massage, then the masseuse left and Lida took over for the last five minutes. She had very powerful hands."

"Lida?"

"No, no. The masseuse. Lida has gentle hands. That's a surprise, isn't it? Lida has those terrific arms and those broad hands, but she's so gentle. —Roll over. I'll do your upper back."

I turned over.

Erin began kneading my shoulders, the back of my neck. "How do you like it?" she asked.

"I like it fine. But I like that other thing we do better."

Little by little, Erin pushed her hands up the back of my neck and into my hair, pressing her fingers into my scalp. "I loved it when Lida did this. Don't you love this?"

"It's all right, I guess."

Erin paused and on the back of my neck I felt the softest kiss ever, but lingering.

"Did Lida do that, too?" I murmured.

"Yes," said Erin, kissing me again on the side of my neck, "Yes," on the nape, "Yes," on the other side. "Like that."

"Are you kidding?"

"No. She did just what I'm doing to you. What do you think about that?"

"I don't know what to think."

"At first it felt strange, knowing it was Lida. But if I didn't think about Lida — I mean, if I didn't think about Lida being a woman — it felt lovely. She kept on that way, not insistent but every now and then another kiss. And if I just took the feeling and didn't think about it, it felt blissful." Erin ceased rubbing my neck, seemed to pause as if she were about to say something.

"And?"

"And after a while I felt foolish pretending it wasn't Lida or that Lida wasn't a woman and I just let it happen."

"And what happened?"

"Not what you think. She just went on and finished the massage and I got up and got dressed and we went on talking the same as ever." Erin leaned down against my back, her leg inside my leg, her breast against my shoulder blade.

"And here you are," I said.

"If it had been any other woman, it would have given me the creeps. But Lida has that direct way of looking at you and touching you and she's so unashamed. While I was getting dressed she looked at my breasts and began to talk about how when she was a kid all her girlfriends began to have real breasts before she did, and how she waited and waited for hers to grow. And when they came they were small and by then her friends had big breasts, but hers never caught up."

"She feels free around you. She likes you."

In back of me, Erin began to slide her leg against the inside of my leg. "Yeah. Well. I think she likes you even better. When Lida was finished massaging my neck she told me I was beautiful, una bella figura, and that sort of thing. I was real smug about that. I keep forgetting how vain I am. Then she asked me is Bart that beautiful — only she called you Bartolomeo — and before I could answer she went on to tell me how beautiful she supposed you were under those clothes. She went on about you for quite a while. Now what you think about that?" she asked, her weight on my back and her warm breath at my ear.

"I don't think about it. Especially now I don't think about it."

Erin had begun to stroke the inside of my thigh. "Do you think she has small breasts?" she murmured, her lips on my ear.

"I never noticed." Erin's story and her smooth insistent caresses were making me hot. "But yours are perfect," I said.

"You think so?"

"Everybody thinks so."

"You and who else?" she asked, sliding her hand rhythmically higher now.

"Hollis has his eye on you."

"How do you like this?" she asked, stroking with her nails now.

"I like it."

"So do I. And I'm here and she's not."

"This is getting uncomfortable. I'm hard."

"I hope you are."

"Let me try something," I said.

We made love again and this time it wasn't an explosive rush. It was slow and steady, heat adding to heat, like yellow-hot metal in a forge when it's folded back and beaten into itself. We turned and turned again in our love making, in our new leisure, and just as I knelt to enter her she turned yet once more, showing me her long back. Her lips were parted but soundless and her eyes were shut — there was no telling what was going on in her head. And I took her that way, looking down on her shimmering skin and the smooth nape of her neck, and I thought of Lida's hands spanning that immaculate flesh, Lida's fingers and the heels of her hands kneading those long muscles as if she, too, were here, and that's when everything gathered and came. Then it was another sort of bliss to lie there, stilled again, so the only motion in the room was at the window where the curtain lifted softly and languidly in a breeze just once.

That evening we cut across a freshly mowed hay field to one of the side roads and walked into town and ate at the first place we came to, which happened to be The Silver Star, just an ordinary diner furnished with Monel metal and blue plastic. We had left the hotel late and by the time we reached the diner we were starved. At that point everything tasted superb and we gorged ourselves. While we were tearing at the hamburgers, Erin remarked that it was odd how people never lost their appetite for food, not unless they were sick.

"What's so odd about that?" I asked her.

"I mean, they go on having this hunger and then satisfying it and then having it again and so on till they die — this hunger for food," she emended, wiping her chin.

"So?"

"But that doesn't happen with sex. People don't go on that way forever with sex. They get over it."

As soon as I had got down my mouthful, I told her

that sex and food weren't alike, that a lot of people went a lifetime without sex, but nobody ever went very long without food.

"In other words, you think it's natural for people to outgrow sex." Her voice had an edgy, accusatory tone.

"What do you mean, *in other words*? I never said anything remotely like that."

"Do you think you could live without sex?" she asked abruptly. She took up her mug and drank, but kept her eyes on me the whole time to see exactly how I answered.

I couldn't figure what she was after. I said it was a trick question, told her she would damn me if I said yes and damn me if I said no.

So she promptly asked another. "Did you ever make love so completely that afterward you didn't care if you ever made it again? I mean, you felt like you were completely gone?"

I laughed and said, "That's the way I feel every time."

"It doesn't always work that way for me," she said flatly.

"God was unfair to women."

"I'd like to make love for hours and hours," she said, her voice oddly matter of fact. "I'd like to do it for days and days until I didn't care about it anymore. I'd like to try that."

"All right, why don't we try it?"

She paused, a handful of French fries held in mid air, and looked to see if I were serious. "To discover how long we could last?"

"Yes."

"How long do you think we could go on?"

"Maybe forever."

Erin laughed and said, "Oh, sure!" and began to eat the fries. "Forever is a long time," she said later, thinking back.

"That's what good about it."

She had turned to gaze out the window at the cars going by on the road, and now she turned back and smiled at me with such tenderness and put her hand to mine on the table and laced our fingers together. I felt my bones melt. Erin didn't say a word.

"Topology is the study of the properties of geometrical configurations that are invariant under transformation," I said.

"What in the world brought that to mind?"

"For years I turned to mathematics as a refuge."

"Is that what you're doing now?" she asked.

"No. That's what's amazing. I haven't thought about mathematics since I saw you on the street. That's what I was thinking just now."

"I turn to books for solace. Or I turn to writing."

"Mathematics was my refuge from life," I told her. "But it was never a solace."

It was evening when we left The Silver Star diner to walk back to the hotel. The sun had crept down close to the horizon, and the light came low across the fields to catch the trees and fill the air with a pale amber haze. The mown hay had a sweet scent to it. "Why does that lovely odor make me feel sad?" Erin said. The August day was long, but not like the long, long days of late June or July. And the margin of our road had a tattered edge of soiled Queen Anne's Lace and faded blue chicory, and where the road sank down to a shallow dale we walked through a pool of chill air that reminded us of autumn coming on. Back in our hotel room the talk turned to mathematics again, because Erin wanted to know what I was trying to find or what I was hoping to demonstrate, and eventually I was telling her or lecturing her or boring her about singularities, those points where something changes abruptly from one state to another, and about mathematical ways of describing those points, and about mathematical ways of describing things which didn't actually change, no matter how much they appeared to be deformed, and about my trying to find a method to link those mathematical expressions. "But this is *foolish*," I said, breaking off.

"Why? Because I can't follow what you're saying the first time around?"

"No," I said. "It's foolish because I've lost interest in the enterprise. I went to that conference hoping to get stimulated, hoping to get aroused, but nothing happened. It left me cold. The whole business leaves me cold. You know what makes a good mathematician? An obsession with mathematics. And I don't have it."

"Well, sometimes I lose my interest in writing. I go dry. But that doesn't mean it's foolish."

I don't know how long we wrangled about writing and mathematics and I can't recall anything of what we said. The conversation grew increasingly abstract, as if by our constant hammering we had beaten the subject to the thinness of air, or maybe we had approached it so closely that the smallest interstices had loomed like canyons and we had fallen in, fallen into nothingness. The conversation had a will and a direction of its own, and I began to worry that we would never reach a place were it would be natural for us to undress and go to bed together. Then Erin stood up, saying, "Are we going to make love or are we going to talk all night?" and pulled her jersey over her head. I stepped out of my pants and threw my shirt over the lamp to douse the light somewhat. A soft *click* or *snap* came from the shadowy end of the room, startling us.

We had fallen quiet as we undressed and now we stood as still as statues — Erin with a foot on the floor and a knee on the bed, I with my hand on her arm. The door that connected our room to the Lords' room looked back at us from the shadows with passive indifference. Erin had turned cautiously and put her mouth to my ear to whisper when we heard it again — a snap or slap or crack — maybe the sound of something yielding under weight, or of wood burning in a fireplace. Erin slid her knee from the bed. We padded noiselessly to the dark end of the room and peeped through the narrow gap along our door's edge. On the Lords' side their door must have swung wide open, for right at hand we could see the satin-paneled folding screen just where it had stood for the past two days, though Hollis's robe — which had been draped over the top this morning — that robe was gone now. And beyond the edge of the screen we could spy deep into the rosy chamber to the fireplace with its antique marble mantel and, above it, the large mirror in the fancy gilded frame. There was a whisper of flames and the crack of burning wood, but the fireplace was empty and the whisper of flames became an amorous murmur, the murmur of Lida's voice, throaty and soft. Then it was silent. Lida walked stiffly to the fireplace in a trim black riding jacket and slender black riding boots, her naked flanks stark white against the black. I felt dizzy, as if the breath had been knocked out of me. She set a half-empty whiskey glass on the mantel and took up the riding crop which lay there. I wanted to look and not look at the same time, my attention skittering from her luminous buttocks to the tightly braided knot of her hair, to her lethal high-heel boots, to the pinched waist of her black velvet jacket, to her buttocks again, to the soft shadows beneath the heavy curves of her flesh. She nervously snatched up the glass and drained it, then strode jerkily back beyond the screen, her face flushed. The little stage was empty, but I couldn't pull myself away. Beside me Erin seemed to forget to draw breath, for we heard a little jingling sound and the creak of leather, and now came harsh and secret whispers and the rhythmic whack of the riding crop. We knew it was Hollis being whacked and I wanted to slink off, sick with shame. The heat of Erin's cheek burned me where it touched against mine, our faces pressed to the crack beside the door. The riding crop whacked louder and more rapidly, then Lida barked a command, gave a voluptuous groan. Her reflection heaved into the mirror — head, jacketed torso, gleaming white flanks — a glaze of sweat on her cheek and neck as she pulled tight the reins and twisted about, panting, whipping her invisible mount harder and still faster. I slid my hand blindly between Erin's warm thighs and shoved against her underpants, the cloth so wet my hand jerked back. She pulled down the soaked garment, yanked it off awkwardly one foot and then the other, hobbled and stumbling across the room toward the bed. She sprawled on her back with her legs open, her eyes watering as if from the heat of her own cheeks while I plunged my fingers deeper and deeper, grinding the heel of my hand against her slippery flesh. She had her fists in my hair and was pulling when I mounted.

Afterward I took a scalding shower to cleanse and punish myself. When I came out of the bathroom Erin was curled naked in the wicker chair, her knees drawn up to her chin and her eyes like stones. She was staring out the window at the black horizon and was smoking a cigarette. "We've got to quit these people," she said, her voice small.

"Tomorrow," I assured her.

"Yes. Tomorrow."

10

IT WAS RAINY the next morning and none of us had
much to say as we drove out of Saratoga. I had been
trying to think about my busted car in Albany and
what to do about it. Hollis turned on the windshield
wipers and paid attention to the wet road. Lida gazed
sleepily out the window. Erin and I sat in back. It was a
soft drizzle and I felt that it actually comforted all of us
to have it this way, now that we were leaving. The trees
and fields were a hazy green and the sky the color of
tarnished silver. It was pleasant to look at the vague
scenery and not to peer into the character of Hollis or
Lida, most pleasant not to think what kind of people they
were. I didn't have a category for Hollis, but Lida reminded me of certain European women I had met: she
had their supervisory flair and authoritative sensuality,
and I was growing tired of it. Later the sky brightened
and we began to talk. Lida told us about the exhibit of
paintings and photographs they had gone to look at yesterday. She said she felt two contrary ways about Georgia O'Keeffe. On the one hand she thought O'Keeffe's
paintings were too stark, the forms of hills and flowers
too simple, too purified. And on the other hand she admired the way O'Keeffe made those plain curves and
folds into huge vulvas.

"What did you say?" Erin asked, startled.

"A woman's vulva," Lida said, turning to face us,
her strong hand on the top of her car seat. "The folds of
the hills and the petals of the flowers take the shape of
the labia. But O'Keeffe paints them so dramatically and

openly that no one notices what they really are. She paints a flower so it fills a whole canvas."

I really didn't want to hear any more. Hollis contradicted her, muttering that a lot of critics had noticed what they looked like.

"She asserts her womanhood. She celebrates a woman's sex," Lida explained to us, ignoring Hollis.

Hollis interrupted to say O'Keeffe always denied that her flowers and landscapes had a sexual meaning.

Lida went on undeflected. "She paints a woman's sexual parts and she makes them beautiful. I like that. I admire the woman. — It's a mystery to me why she stayed married to Stieglitz and his little camera," she told us.

Hollis spoke up again, said O'Keeffe and Stieglitz loved each other and that's why they stayed married. That might be a mystery to Lida, he added.

"She went to New Mexico every summer. Without him," Lida said sharply, jerking back to Hollis. "She had to get away to survive!"

Hollis gave an irritable shrug. "Life is difficult. They loved each other," he repeated.

"I don't know what that means, coming from you," Lida said.

We fell into an uncomfortable silence. I had known that Georgia O'Keeffe was a painter, but I couldn't recall what her paintings looked like, and I had not even heard of this Stieglitz until yesterday and, I'm sorry to say, I had confused him with the mathematician and electrical engineer Steinmetz. I was trying to think of a good way to change the subject when Erin asked how the two artists had met. Hollis said that Stieglitz had owned a gallery in the city and had showed O'Keeffe's work and that's how they got started. "Did they have children?" Erin asked. Yes, Hollis told her, the man liked children.

"No. No children," Lida announced briskly, turning

to us.

"He had a child by his first wife," Hollis said, raising his voice to talk over Lida. *"He loved children."*

A deep horn blasted in back of us and a massive truck thundered slowly past, veiling our windows with a sheet of water. As the windshield cleared we watched the truck go by the car ahead of us, giving it a glancing touch on the way. Hollis began to slow down. The car ahead was sliding lazily toward the edge of the pavement, gliding along until its right wheels touched the rain-soaked earth of the shoulder, whereupon it hopped clumsily into the air and plowed down the shallow embankment and vanished behind us. Hollis eased onto the shoulder and came to a halt.

We ran down the little embankment. The vehicle, an old brown station wagon with steam drifting up from the hood, had crashed head first into a granite outcropping. I peered through the muddy glass of the driver's door while Hollis ran to the passenger side. The front seat was folded forward against the dashboard. "It's empty," I said, tugging at the door. "Oh, shit," Hollis said from the other side. At that moment I saw the driver, his forearm and head crammed impossibly between the steering post and the rim of the wheel. I let go the door, not wanting to deal with the mess, and ran around to Hollis. The door on that side was wide open and Hollis was crouched beside a body which lay by the rear wheel. It was an old woman who watched him, her cheek resting on her hand on the deep soggy grass, dazed, blood seeping from her hairline and across her forehead. "Everything is going to be all right," he assured her, his voice ragged but authoritative. The radio was humming. I reached into the car, squeezing my hand between the seat and the dashboard to turn off the ignition key.

Lida came running down the embankment with Erin at her side. "We stopped a couple of cars and told them to get help," they said. Hollis and I pulled at the driver's door, but I was praying it wouldn't budge, fearful of what we'd find. Hollis wrenched it open and gently pried back the seat. "Can you hear me?" he asked the man in the wheel. For a moment nothing happened, then the driver slowly drew his hand out from wheel and cautiously pulled back his head. "Easy does it," Hollis told him. He slumped in the seat, an older man with his face smashed and his eyes still shut, his wire spectacle frames driven into his flesh. His lips were moving, saying over and over, "Josie? Are you okay, Josie?" Hollis carefully peeled the wire frames from the man's face and began to talk to him. I walked around to the other side. The woman was seated on the soaked grass, weeping and asking for her purse. The misty rain was beginning to dilute the blood that crept from her gray hair, spreading a large pink blot across her forehead. Erin came up with the purse and gave it to her. Lida had taken off her sweater — the same big white sweater Erin had borrowed — and now she knelt in the muddy grass beside the woman and folded the sweater tenderly around the woman's shoulders, keeping her arm there. "Now your purse is in your lap and help is on the way," she told the woman, touching her cheek with a caress. "What's your name?"

Help did arrive, eventually. A State Police car pulled up behind the Jaguar and an officer in a neatly pressed blue uniform came down, walking carefully across the marshy turf as if he might plunge through it. He asked us what had happened, counted the injured, looked inside the station wagon, then went back to his car to radio for help. We decided to stay and wait. The misty rain stopped. By the time the ambulance came, the old man was in shock, his face gray. The woman, Josie, had become frightened, so Lida held her hand and walked beside her stretcher while it was being carried to the ambulance. After the ambulance sped off, Lida folded up her white sweater and we got into the Jaguar and finished our trip to Albany. Each of us was preoccupied in a private way by what had happened, so conversation went by fits and starts. Certainly I didn't say much. I had stood around helpless and had given nothing while Hollis and Lida had moved instinctively to comfort the injured, to stop the bleeding and calm the fear. I was ashamed of myself.

We arrived in Albany around noon and drove directly to the railroad station. I went in with Erin while she checked her schedule, adjusted her old ticket. The next good train to Manhattan would leave late in the afternoon. I had emptied my checking account while we were in Saratoga and now had only enough cash to pay for lunch and a bit more. As we left the ticket window I asked if she had enough money. "Barely. But when I get to the city I'll take the subway. I don't need to take a cab," she told me. "Anyway, if I had money I'd stay here while you got that damn car fixed." We walked along without talking. The huge station was almost deserted and our footsteps echoed in the stagnant, hollow air. I kept trying to think of a way we could stay together for a couple of more days, but I couldn't think and my heart felt like a hole in my chest.

"Our bodies are so frail, Bart." She was looking down at the palm of her hand and now she turned it over and began flexing her fingers. "This stuff can get ripped or broken, just like that. It scares me."

I put my arm around her and pushed open one of the big doors and we went outside. Hollis drove us uptown to the street where I had left my car and there it was, snug against the curb, looking like a real Volkswagon and not at all like a rudderless piece of junk. A short while later we learned from a phone book that the nearest VW garage was located somewhere outside the city at a traffic circle conveniently remote from Albany, Schenectady and Troy. "You can try the garage where we go with the Jag," Hollis suggested. "At least it's right here in the city." So we drove to Van Schaik's Foreign Automobile & Sports Car Repairs, a small garage at the far end of a cinder yard packed with expensive cars. Hollis went in to do the talking and five minutes later he returned with a mechanic at his side, a skeptical looking man who studied me without a word while wiping his hands on a filthy orange rag. "This is Hank Van Schaik," he said. "He'll tow your car back here and look it over." I climbed into the tow truck with silent Van Schaik and directed him to my car while Hollis followed in the Jaguar. We stood by while Van Grumpy hooked the car to his truck and hauled it away, then we went to that eatery where we all had met three days ago.

For the first time I saw that Lida's skirt had a huge mud stain where she had knelt to take care of Josie, and I noticed that Hollis's shirt had three brown spots of blood, like medals, beside his chest pocket. At lunch Erin told us comic stories about her apartment mates, but the thought of her away in New York made me feel lousy and I was a lot happier when we began talking about politics and Eisenhower. Then we drove back to Foreign Automobiles & Sports Car Repairs. Erin and I went in. Van Schaik was bent over an exploded MG engine, the orange rag sticking out of his back pocket. A mechanic informed me that the roller steering gear on my car was broken and that they could have it ready by the day after tomorrow. I said I wouldn't be able to pay for it till I got back to Boston. Van Schaik, not looking up or turning around, grunted that it would be okay to send him a check. That surprised me. Erin and I walked out to where the Lords were waiting placidly in their Jaguar.

"Where to?" Hollis asked me as I came up.

I had been trying to think about this all morning but had gotten nowhere. I could go to a Western Union office and call my parents, ask my father to wire me enough money for two days at a cheap hotel in Albany. But another two hours here in Boredom, New York, would drive me crazy and two more days would kill me. Or maybe I could borrow a little from Hollis, enough for a ticket. Then I could ride the train to Boston and visit my savings bank and two days later I could ride the train back to Albany, pay the repair bill and drive back to Boston. I had been back and forth over this ever since getting of bed. I looked around for Erin and found she had stopped to scratch the head of Van Schaik's elderly mongrel dog. I could no more part from Erin than I could tear the heart out of my chest and throw it away.

"I don't know," I answered.

The sun had come out and the streets were drying.

"I hope you won't mind if we make a suggestion," Hollis said.

11

WE WENT WITH the Lords to their place in the Berkshires. Hollis and Lida said we could stay with them until my car was ready, then they would give us a lift back to Albany. They said they didn't have extra beds, but they had a couple of sleeping bags and plenty of space, and if Erin and I didn't mind camping on the floor we could all lie under the same roof for two nights. It was entirely up to Erin and me, they said, but they hoped we'd say yes. So Lida and Erin went to buy groceries, Hollis filled the gas tank, I called my father and mother, told them I was still in New York and not to worry if I didn't answer my phone for the next few days. Then we hopped into the car and crossed the Hudson out of Albany.

Hollis drove down along the river for a while, then turned toward the mountains. The road curved and dipped and climbed through the green and brown countryside. Sometimes the trees would crowd against the car and other times they would fall back a few paces or ebb entirely, leaving wide acres of rolling brown fields, then suddenly they would rush back to the road, submerging us in green twilight. Hollis said the whole country around there had been well populated at one time, but people had been moving away for the past hundred years and wilderness had reclaimed most of the land. It was lonesome, as if the last inhabitant had moved out just a while ago. Eventually we went through a place called Chatham Bridge or East Corners or something like that — a general store, two rusted gas pumps and a boarded-up hotel — and from there we began an abrupt climb up a slope of wooded hills on an oiled dirt road, then up a loose dirt road and finally along a pair of worn car ruts. We passed a shallow cellar hole and turned off the road. "The farm house is gone," Lida explained. "We live up there in the barn."

"This is it," Hollis said. "Home. More or less."

The car rolled to a stop beside a faded red barn which stood all alone at the crest of the hill. We got out and I was astonished at the silence. There was only this solitary barn in this upland field and no sound at all.

"It's so peaceful here," Erin said. "It's so *quiet*. No wonder you hate to give it up. I'd never give it up."

The Lords didn't reply. Lida merely frowned at the horizon, Hollis looked down and knocked some gravel aside with the toe of his shoe. "Well," they said at last, turning to each other as if to business. "Let's take in the groceries."

We picked up our things and went in through a door in the side. The Lords had completely remade the interior. From the outside it had looked like an ordinary barn — the gable end that faced the road had a huge sliding door in it, and around the back the land fell away and there was another door which lead into the cellar. But inside they had built a wall and turned the front half of the barn into Lida's studio and the back half into living quarters.

The apartment was a simple place, practically one big room, filled with daylight. The back wall was mostly windows or glass doors and gave a clean view over the fields and woods. When you turned around you took in the whole apartment, the ice box and kerosene stove on one side, the bed with an Indian blanket on the other, and some sheep skins on the floor. Everything was open to everything else and I wondered where we were going to lay the sleeping bags. "Where's the bathroom?" Erin asked. The bathroom was behind that door by the kitchen sink, and Hollis told us how many times we had to work the pump handle to refill the tank. "And there's an outhouse down by the woods, if you really want to get rustic," Lida added with a laugh.

I asked Hollis was there anything I could give him a hand with. Lida broke in to remind me they were going to sell the place and working on it wouldn't make sense, but Hollis decided there were some boulders he still wanted to move, a two-man job, down by the stream. I wanted to work, so that was fine by me. We went out and he gave me a six-foot length of iron pipe and took another for himself and we walked down across the back field to the stream. It was just a rivulet now in August and you could jump across it if you took a good running start, but the Lords had dug out the banks and had damned the stream with rocks to make a fair size bathing pool. Hollis wanted to shift some of the boulders around the edge, so we took off our shoes and socks and rolled up our pants and got to work. It was a harder chore than I had expected — both of us heaving and groaning and gasping — but it felt good to work up a sweat. When we were finished, Hollis dragged the pipes up to the barn and returned with a couple of towels. We took a quick skinny-dip in the pool, my eyes shying away from Hollis's lean paunch and pendulous penis, then we dried off and pulled on our clothes. I was reminded of Erin and Lida at the Saratoga baths together, and wondered why women found it easier than men to grasp or caress each other's flesh. But, I told myself, maybe that's only what men think. We didn't bother to put on our socks and shoes, but went up to dinner barefoot, and that was just as well, because Erin and Lida had taken off their shoes, too. The touch of the wood floor beneath our feet came back from long ago — like a good childhood memory, Erin remarked.

"Children go barefoot all the time," Lida said, as we sat down to eat. "That's why they're happier than adults. They have the feeling of freedom. If I had children, I'd let them go barefoot all the time." Her face hardened an instant, as if someone were going to contradict her.

"I made the salad," Erin told us cheerfully. "Lida cooked the sausage and sliced the bread."

"Bless this food to our use and us to your service," Hollis said, tipping his head briefly toward each of the women in turn.

I asked about the guns leaning in the corner, a mammoth double-barreled shotgun and a couple of slender rifles, including one that appeared to have a hexagonal barrel and an engraved breech. "Hunting?"

"Too dangerous," he said. "People come up from the city and bang away at anything that moves — cows, automobiles, trees swaying in the wind — and if they can't see something to shoot at they'll shot at noises. Those are antiques, but I have a pistol if you'd like some target practice."

"After dinner Hollis will take you out back and you two can try hitting an old coffee can at fifty feet," Lida told me, putting her hand to my wrist.

As a matter of fact, after dinner Lida and Erin went down to the pool while Hollis and I did try the pistol. The land sloped down to the stream on the left and to a woods on the right. Hollis had put in a solitary fence post as a boundary marker at the far right corner of the acreage and he occasionally used the post for target practice, too. Now he came along with the pistol in one hand and, in the other, an old galvanized bucket that had been shot all out of shape. He managed to get the bucket to balance more or less upright on the post so we could shoot downhill, our misses tearing through the brush and burying themselves in the dirt. The pistol was an old Army .45 automatic — big, square, ungainly. "I used to know how to strip that thing and put it together again," I said.

"Korea?" he asked.

"Reserve," I said.

"An officer," he said, smiling. "If you had one of these."

I shrugged, hoping to show indifference.

"I got this on the black market in Venice in 1945," he said. He shoved the clip in. "I wanted one because the officers carried them, the officers and the MPs. I wanted to try firing the damn thing. The story was it would stop anyone you hit, no matter where you hit him. I thought it would come in handy."

"Sure, if you hit him," I said. "But who can hit anything with it?"

"Yeah. That's the joke."

Hollis gave me the pistol. I had forgotten how heavy it was and it sank in my hand. I composed myself. I breathed, aimed, sighted and squeezed, just as I had been taught to do. The .45 banged and jumped, sending a satisfying jolt back through my arm. I had missed, of course. I brought my arm down and slowly fired again. I emptied the entire clip without hitting a damn thing. "I think it's time we advanced on the enemy," I said, handing over the pistol.

"It's notoriously inaccurate," he said. He put in a fresh clip. His first two shots missed, but I suspected he was just being polite to me. His third hit the post. "You're right, we need to advance." He walked a few paces forward and fired the remaining shots rather carelessly, missing. "Try it from here," he said.

My third shot grazed the side of the bucket. It teetered around moment, almost got its balance back, then gave up and toppled off the post. "I think I'll quit now," I told him.

Hollis put the bucket on the post, came back to my side and allowed himself to hit the thing square with his next shot. We were still taking turns when the women came up from the pool. They had pulled on jerseys and wrapped towels around their waists, and Lida had another towel draped about her neck.

"Want a crack at it?" Hollis asked them.

"The mosquitoes are beginning to come out," Lida said. "It's time for you guys to quit. It's getting dusky down there. Come on, Hollis."

"Take a shot," he insisted, holding the butt of the .45 out to her. "Show them what you can do."

Lida stood passively with her fists clamped to the towel ends that hung from around her neck and she looked at Hollis. The jersey was stuck to her breasts and belly in dark wet patches and you could guess at the athletic body underneath. "I'll take a shot if you'll quit and come in," she said at last.

"Fine. There's three rounds left. Empty it."

Lida planted her feet, closed her left hand on her right wrist, raised the gun and fired. The bucket sailed from the post, crashed and rolled noisily on the ground, then spun around wildly as her second and third shot hit it. She handed Hollis the pistol and the empty clip, a flicker of distaste about her mouth.

"Oh, wow," Erin said. "Where'd you learn to shoot like that?"

Lida didn't answer right away. "Let's go in and leave them to the mosquitoes," she said, taking Erin's arm.

Hollis gave a short laugh. "She says she doesn't like to, but you see how well she does it," he told me. Then he sighed and said, "Well, I suppose it's getting a little shadowy down there and we might as well quit."

I wasn't a good shot, but the .45 had come to feel both strong and graceful in my hand and, frankly, I was sorry to stop. Hollis squinted at the fading sky while I caught the summery scent of gun smoke and cosmoline and I was reminded not of the Army, but of when I was a kid watching my father and uncles trap shooting against the sunset on Cape Cod. We walked down to inspect the post and the bucket one last time, then headed up to the barn.

Later Hollis and I stood on the balcony outside the glass and watched the sun go down. He remarked that Saratoga was one of the oldest social places on this continent, but out here there was no society at all, nothing but nature. Little by little the field got dark so you couldn't even make out the vegetable patch. Then the sky faded away except for the bright specks where stars came out, and when I looked around I discovered there were no lights on any of the hills, no sign of habitation anywhere, not even a patch of sky-glow to suggest a distant city beyond the horizon. It was getting cool, so we went inside. Lida and Erin had pulled on their clothes and lighted the oil lamps, including the big pewter one that hung over the dinner table where they were sitting down to play cards. The other table, the square one that Hollis used as a desk, held an old typewriter and a jumble of books and photos. Half the volumes were lying face up and flat open on another layer of books, and the books that were shut had other books tucked inside for bookmarks, though I did see one that used a pen to keep a place and another had a wristwatch hanging out by its strap and a couple more had table knives. Hollis made a pass at straightening up the mess. He'd pick up a volume and look around to lay it someplace else, but he'd always end up by setting it back carefully where he'd found it.

In addition to their library of classy art books, the Lords had a dozen volumes on house construction and a shelf of paperback novels, many of them in French or Italian. I came across *The Stranger*, a novel my literary friends had liked to argue about when I was in college. My French wasn't too good, but the book wasn't even a half inch thick, so I thought I'd give it a try. Erin and Lida were having a fine time slapping cards onto the table and crying *gin*, and Hollis was rearranging the top layer of his desk, and I was lounging on the floor beside an oil lamp, reading. I hadn't felt so contented in years. I admit that after a while I began skipping ahead in the novel. It was about a man who shot another man, but it didn't say why. When we got chill, Hollis kindled a fire in the Franklin stove and Lida made a pot of coffee and Erin, peeling an orange, came over to see what I was reading. I was happy to give up on the book. Lida spread a few more cushions on the floor and we sat around talking of this and that, just enjoying each other's company. "When I was in college one of my dreams was to have a place of my own and live like this with friends, drinking coffee and talking all through the night," Erin said.

Lida smiled and set the pot down on the floor, saying, "You should go to Paris or Rome." Hollis was lying propped on his elbow, reading the label on a wine bottle, and Lida knelt behind him to massage his shoulders. She began to tell us about her school days in Trieste during the war. She was matter of fact about it and even made jokes, but it sounded grim. The last time she had seen her father was at the station in Trieste when he boarded the train for Prague. Whether he was killed by Nazis or Communists or by American bombs, she never was able to find out. Hollis had gone to put away the wine and come back with a bottle of brandy and we added that to the coffee. It turned out that Hollis had been with the Fifth Army and had met Lida over there in 1945. "He nearly ran me over in his jeep," Lida said. "He was driving a couple of officers someplace, but he backed up and jumped out and apologized."

"Love at first sight," Erin said.

Maybe it was, but Lida didn't tell us so. "He went his way, I went mine," she said at last.

"But I went back on foot at the same hour next day, intending to find her," Hollis said. "And there she was, standing on the curb at the same spot, watching the military traffic drive past."

"Looking for him," Lida admitted, as if it had been a mistake.

"In the same blue and white summer dress, so I wouldn't miss her," Hollis added.

"One of my two summer dresses," said Lida, shifting restlessly. She snatched up the coffee pot, took it to the wood stove to re-heat it.

Lida had been in that part of the city on her way to

British Headquarters, hoping for a job as a translator or typist or clerk of some sort. That was her mother's idea. Through the last years of the war, through all the fighting in Italy, her mother had worried that some authority would order them out of Trieste, send them back to Prague to vanish like her husband. After the Italians surrendered to the Allies, the Germans seized power and made life even more chaotic and dangerous, and after the Germans fled, the barbarian Yugoslavs announced their intention to take over the city. Now the English and the Americans had arrived to assert their authority and now, her mother said, was the moment for these two women to show themselves. Their first move would be to get jobs with the British and make the acquaintance of some officers who knew the bureaucrats who could deliver the right papers, because with the right papers you could go anywhere and without them you became a refugee and ended up in a Godforsaken mud camp. While Lida was telling us this, Hollis was over at the shadowy desk, opening and shutting some little drawers. Now he came back with a small framed photograph and a loose snapshot. "Here she is," he said, giving them to Erin.

The camera had caught her from the waist up — a young woman outside a big paneled doorway, smiling and squinting just a little in the harsh black-and-white sunshine. The wide cheek bones were not as distinct in the photo as they were now, and the smile was wasn't as full and open, but it was Lida all right. "Oh, your hair is the same as people in this country wore it during the war," Erin said. The other photo showed Lida with a woman. The two had linked arms and were standing shoulder to shoulder in front of a railing by the sea, and both women were smiling broadly at the camera. The other woman was better looking, stood straighter, displayed a more receptive body, and it was only after I had lingered over the picture that I saw she was years older, too. "This other woman in the picture —" Erin hesitated.

"You were going to say we look like sisters?" asked Lida with half a smile.

"Your mother," I said.

"Thank you, Bart. Yes, my mother," she said.

"You inherit her beauty," Erin murmured, studying the snapshot. "And you improve on it," she added.

Her mother lived in London now. She had stayed behind in Italy when Lida left for the United States, and six months later she had moved to England. About ten years ago she had come to the States with the thought of settling down in New York, but the visit had not worked out well and she had returned to London, remaining there ever since. I examined the snapshot and thought she looked about as old as Lida or Hollis looked right now — younger than Hollis, I decided. I asked Lida what her mother was like.

"Oh —" She opened her arms, shrugged, dropped her arms. "What can I say? She's European. Anyway, we were very close."

"Like sisters," Erin suggested.

"More like impossible friends," Hollis said, his voice crisp.

"Hollis thinks my mother was a bad influence on me. And maybe he's right. Maybe she was." But Lida said this lightly, making it clear that it no longer mattered to her.

I don't know how long we went on. When Lida talked about Trieste during the war she spoke with the same energy and the same gestures as always — well, almost the same as always — but in addition there was a hard flippancy in her manner and it was obvious there were things she didn't want to talk about. Erin had pillowed her head on my thigh, insisting that she wasn't tired and wasn't sleepy, but when I began to comb my fingers through her hair she shut her eyes anyway. Lida brought out the sleeping bags, and Erin and I unrolled them in front of the wood stove between the tables. We zippered the sleeping bags together to make a single quilted bed for the both of us. Lida blew out the big pewter oil lamp and turned down the one beside their bed. It was too shadowy for us to see into their corner of the room, too shadowy for them to see into ours. After a while their light went out and I blew out our lamp, too.

I had not thought of making love. I mean, I had thought about it and then tried to put it out of mind, because I figured that Erin wouldn't want to and neither would I, not with the Lords in the same room twenty feet away. But now she turned toward me, rolled half onto me, and her skin was startlingly warm. I put my arm around her shoulders and whispered, "Do you want to?" She didn't answer, but kissed my mouth, slid her leg between mine and began to rub against me. When I asked again did she want to, she shook her head no. She had clamped her legs on my leg and kept rubbing while she whispered, "What do you think they're doing? Do you think — they're doing it? Oh, Jesus." I said I didn't care, said I was getting hard and let's do something. Erin's mouth was at my ear but I couldn't tell if her breath was making words or if she were panting. She felt hot and slippery against my thigh. "Don't know," she gasped at last. "Excites me. They're so close. Oh, Jesus Jesus — " Then she rolled away and about a minute later I heard her breathing grow deep and slow. I lay there aroused and resentful, but before long I fell asleep, too.

12

THE NEXT MORNING I got up, pulled on my under shorts, picked up a towel and nearly crashed
into the Lords at the table — said good morning
to them — then went into the bathroom. When I came
out I noticed for the first time that Lida's eyes were wa-
tery and red from weeping and that Hollis, across from
her, was gazing beyond her in morose silence. I turned
to Erin just as she slipped past me into the bathroom.
"Sit down, Bart," Lida said, clearing her throat of tears.
"Would you like some pancakes?"

I pretended to wipe at my neck with the towel, said I
could make something for myself, hurriedly turned to
the kitchen counter. I found the bowl of pancake batter
and busied myself whipping it. Lida came over in her
peignoir or kimono or whatever it's called.

"I'll take care of that," she said. "Go keep Hollis company."

I sat down at the table in my under shorts, my towel
still over my shoulder. I didn't know what the hell was
going on.

"Sorry about this," Hollis said. "As you probably
guessed long ago, Lida and I — We're separating."

Erin had returned and when she heard Hollis her face
went blank, as if a light had been switched off.

"As a matter of fact, we had just come from the
lawyer's office when we bumped into you," Hollis said.
He wore only a pair of swim trunks and looked thin in
his nakedness.

Erin sat down cautiously, listening.

"No," I said. "We hadn't guessed."

"Yes. Well. There it is. That's why we had to make the arrangements to sell this place. Common property. I know this place is somewhat remote, off the beaten track and all, but we think it's a nice place and somebody will want it. We have to find the right person to sell to, that's all," he said, rambling. "Lida knows some places, where to advertise. We're not asking a lot. I think we can make back what we put into it." He hesitated and looked at me and at Erin. "What do you think?"

"You mean you're getting a divorce?" Erin asked him, incredulous.

"Lida wants a divorce," he said. "Yes."

Erin opened her mouth as if to say something, then closed it.

"Listen, I'm sorry about this. I really am — " Hollis began apologetically.

"I mean — It's a surprise, is all I mean," Erin told him. Her gaze had darted to Lida, but Lida was busy at the pancake griddle, her back to us.

Hollis turned studiously to his breakfast. Erin and I silently watched him pour maple syrup over his pancakes as if we had never seen it done before. Lida came up with pancakes for me and Erin. "We have real maple syrup," she informed us, her voice husky and her eyes still wet.

In the long silence we could hear from beyond the windows the metallic trill of one cicada and then another. Someone remarked that it meant the weather was going to be especially hot, and I don't recall what we talked about next. I was confused and sorry about the Lords, but also I was hungry and after the first bite I forgot myself and commenced to pitchfork pancakes until my plate was bare. Erin cleaned her plate, too. Lida brought a pot of coffee to the table.

"Why are you guys getting divorced?" Erin asked,

100

her voice skittering unevenly as she tried to get the right tone.

Hollis didn't say anything but raised his eyes to Lida, as if deferring to her.

"That's a long story," Lida said at last.

"No. Please. I want to know," Erin insisted.

I told her that maybe these people wanted their privacy.

Hollis gave a curt laugh. "It's a little late for that," he said.

"But you get along so *well* together," Erin told them. "From the first moment in that restaurant —"

"I was on my way to New York," Lida said flatly. "Hollis was going to return here alone."

"But how could you?"

"The train station was just down the street," Lida reminded her.

And then I remembered suitcase open on the bed in their hotel room when she gave Erin that white sweater to keep off the evening chill. "The suitcase," I said.

"What? Oh. Oh," Erin said, remembering it, too. "You had packed for New York. But if you were really, actually going to split up, why did you want to waste your time on us? I don't *understand.* —This is all *wrong*," she protested, coloring slightly.

"Well, that's the way it happened," Lida said, sighing raggedly. "We had just come from the attorney's office and we were exhausted and we were depressed. Oh, God. Then you two walked in and, oh — you know."

"No, I don't!" Erin said hotly. "I don't know anything anymore. Why did you invite us to join you? You tricked us!"

"That's not true, Erin," she said. "You — We —" Her eyes began to water as if she had been slapped.

Hollis came to her aid, saying, "When I saw Bart — he looked so happy and energetic — I didn't take time to think, I just was happy to see him. And then I thought if he, if you, would come and sit with us we could forget for a while what was happening. And you looked so wonderful, so flushed and expectant. You're full of life, you two, and you don't know what that means."

"We used to be like you," Lida told her, drying her eyes with the heel of her hand. "We used to have a future. People would look at us and see how handsome we were and want to be like us. I knew what they were thinking and I was as vain as you are. Oh, God. People used to be happy around us."

I could never have imagined Lida weeping. She had seemed to take such pride in being self-possessed and now, watching her, I felt my heart being twisted and my eyes began to water. I didn't know what to say.

"Frankly, I don't understand how you can go to a divorce lawyer and then sleep in the same bed together," Erin told her. "And another thing I don't understand is, if you're going to split up and if you want to split up, then why are you in tears?"

"There's a lot of things you don't understand. Life's complicated," Lida said, her eyes still glistening.

Erin slumped back in her chair and blew a fallen sheaf of hair out of her eyes. "All right. All right. Sorry I asked," she said, getting up. "I'll do the dishes."

I cleared the table, then I rolled up our sleeping bags and finally I pulled on a pair of pants. None of us had dressed when we got up, but it seemed I was the only one who felt uncomfortable about it. I went out onto the balcony. A bright wedge of sun lay across the boards, making them hot to my bare feet. I leaned my elbows on the rail and looked at the horizon and tried to figure out how to get through the next twenty-four hours. Erin came onto the balcony and began to unfold one of the canvass chairs. She was still wearing only her underpants and a long, loose jersey.

"Wasn't that an interesting breakfast?" I said.

She laughed briefly. "Lida's right. There's a lot of things I don't understand."

I asked if she could see what the Lords were doing inside.

"Lida's over by the sink, trimming the wicks on the kerosene lamps. I don't know where Hollis is." She came to the rail and looked at the scraggly vegetable patch and the brown fields. "What are we going to do now?" she asked.

I hadn't any idea what to do. "I'd like to heat some water for a shave. I suppose you want to get dressed, don't you?"

Erin shrugged. "Actually, I'd like to lie out here and read a cheap, trashy magazine. A magazine with articles on how to get a perfect tan. My guess is that Lida doesn't have any cheap, trashy magazines. Can you figure out what's going on in their heads?"

"They're getting a divorce. Don't you believe them? I do."

"I know they're getting a divorce. That's the easy part," she said.

"What do you mean?"

"How can they do those things at night when they're already splitting up? They don't just go to bed. You know what I mean, getting into those costumes and doing those things to each other and then, you know, in the hotel room. What can they be thinking of? What can they be feeling?"

I said I didn't know what they were going through, said I felt sorry for them anyway.

"And Lida can be so cruel," Erin continued. "She weeps over breaking up with Hollis, but she's the one who wants to leave. Hollis looks like he's dying by inches, poor man. He's the one I'm sorry for."

"Well, we don't have the whole story," I said.

"We have enough of it."

"I'm going to shave," I told her. "Are you coming in to get dressed?" Frankly, I thought she should cover up a bit.

"No. I'm going to lie out here in the sun. I'm dressed enough to do that."

I went inside. Lida looked over her shoulder and saw me just as she was opening the door to her studio. "Bart, come take a look at my workroom," she said.

The workroom was the other half of the barn. About a dozen of Lida's big wood sculptures stood in there among some odds and ends of furniture, yet the studio looked larger than the living quarters. They had put windows between the wall studs and had cut a huge slanting window overhead, so it seemed a square chunk of sky had fallen through, and we were standing in it. "This is a great place. No wonder you like to work here," I said.

"Yes. Well. We were going to insulate it but we never got around to it. It's hot in summer and cold in winter. But it's nice now," she added indifferently.

Lida was still in her kimono and I had no shirt on. I stuffed my hands in my pockets and stood there, gazing idiotically at her sculptures, her work table and the rows of tools, all the while uncomfortably aware of her body so casually wrapped.

"Walk around. Don't be shy. You can touch anything," she told me, going away to the window.

So here was a polished square post about six feet tall — made of oak, I guessed — and it had a man's face carved in shallow relief up near the top, but nothing else, except down below where his privates might be there dangled a six-inch length of limp garden hose. "This guy has a problem," I said.

Lida was peering into a crumpled cigarette pack and she didn't look up. "That block of wood is the kind of stupid witticism that gets attention in a gallery now-a-days," she said flatly.

I walked around and looked at the other pieces, not knowing what to say about them. Some of her sculptures were roughly hewn slabs of wood with a meaningless array of letters and numerals carved on them, markers for some obscure game or rite, but most of her work took a human shape. I wandered from piece to piece. I didn't actually dislike the stuff. "What do you think?" she asked. I was at the far end of the studio, looking at a smooth female figure that was about my height and not much bigger around than a fence post. Long vertical cracks had opened as the wood dried — or maybe it had been purposely split — and you could see the raw fibers inside being tugged slowly apart.

"I don't care so much for the sign posts, but I like these," I said.

"Those sign posts are supposed to be like stele. Only they don't mean anything. I was infatuated with abstraction when I did those."

I meandered back to Lida who was sitting on a short step-ladder by the work table. There was an unlighted cigarette between her fingers, but the hand lay in her lap as if she had forgotten it. Her shoulders were slumped and the kimono was sagging open a bit. It pained me to see Lida so empty and sad, and at the same time I felt an awkward stirring of desire for her.

"Are you all right?" I asked.

"Oh, yes. I'm all right." She straightened up and shook open her robe and wrapped it more neatly shut. I looked away, the glimpse of her breast still gleaming in memory.

"What's the matter then?" I asked.

"I don't want a divorce any more than Hollis does. But we have to go through with it."

"Why?"

"He says I'm killing him. But I think he's killing himself. I've got to leave. I don't know what else to do." She fell silent.

I searched for something to say. "I like your work." My tongue had gone dry.

She looked at me a while and then said, "Well, I like to do it. I've taken the long way around to human contours, but that's all I want to work on now. That's where the meaning is. The rest is empty form."

Lida's kimono was a bright yellowish color, rather like brass, and the cloth looked slippery. It had sagged open again. I looked back to her eyes and found her watching me. I reached out cautiously to stroke her hair and she lifted her face, rubbed her broad cheek slowly against my hand and then kissed my palm. Her breasts were flat and rather high, and as her robe unwrapped and fell away it disclosed a surprising flourish of tawny hair, amazingly thick and rich to the touch. I had grown obscenely hard and I hated myself, but everything was sliding out of control.

"My breasts are small."

"Your breasts are fine," I told her.

13

AFTERWARD I DIDN'T know what to think or what to do and, as stupid as it sounds, I wasn't even sure how I felt. We had made love on an exercise mat, or maybe it was just an old sofa mattress, and then we lay there side by side for a minute — she on her back and me on my belly. I didn't even know where to look. Lida got up and found her unsmoked cigarette and lit it. By the time I stood and looked, she was sitting naked on the work table with her legs dangling and her ankles crossed. Something in the easy way she sat there made me feel less ashamed, but crazy, too. She took the cigarette from her lips and gave it to me. I took a hasty puff and handed it back, then pulled on my pants. I was about to open the door to the apartment when Lida said, "Don't barge in there. Rattle the door first."

"What?"

"And don't get angry."

"I'm not angry." Then it began to dawn on me.

"I know you're not angry at me. Don't get angry at anybody else," she said.

I yanked the door so furiously it swung out of my hand and crashed into the wall. The place was empty. Hollis was naked on the balcony in the canvas lounge chair where Erin had been sitting. I don't know what my face looked like when I burst out there, but he took one glance and said, "Take it easy, Bart. She's down at the pool. You just missed her."

I jogged down the field toward the pool. I felt rotten for having betrayed Erin and the thought of her with Hollis was like a hole in my chest. She was seated on a rock at the edge of the pool, still in her underpants and jersey. Her knees were pulled under her chin and she was staring glumly into the water. When she heard me coming she jerked around, then scuttled into the pool and hid herself neck-deep in the water, her eyes on me all the while. I stood on the rock out of breath and the sun banged on my head, making me dizzy.

"What do you want?" she asked.

"You —" I broke off.

"What about me?"

"You and Hollis," I began again.

She just kept staring at me, steady and unblinking.

"Oh, hell," I said.

"All right, me and Hollis. What do you want to know?" Her face remained watchful and still, while the sunken length of her hair slowly fanned out like a spreading cloud of ink in the water.

"Nothing," I said at last.

"I didn't plan it," she said defiantly.

"I know, I know."

"The way it happened was —"

"Don't say it. You don't have to say it."

Erin stood up in the water and tugged her drenched jersey over her head and off, then she sank down again and a moment later her hand came to the surface with the soaked wad of her underpants. "Anyway, you were in there with Lida," she muttered.

"So?"

She simply looked at me and waited.

"Do you want details? Is that what you want?" My voice was too loud.

"No. I have a good imagination. I just want you to admit it," she said.

"I admit it. Now what?"

"Now we're even," she said.

"Great. Now we're even. That's great."

Erin spread her jersey and underpants on a rock in the sun, then swam two strokes and rolled onto her back and pulled up under the trees at the other side of the pool. "You might wash it off, at least," she told me.

I unbuckled and pulled off my clothes and eased myself down from the rock for a soak. The water was cool and though there wasn't enough room to really swim, it felt good to splash around, sometimes in the sun and sometimes in the tangled shade of the trees. I don't know how long we stayed there. I was in no rush to get back to the barn, because I didn't have any idea how to behave when we got there. Erin claimed she didn't care about behaving. "Everybody knows what happened, no one is going to pretend," she said. We were sitting on the rocks in the sun, drying off. "I think we should just act natural," she concluded. I said I didn't know what was natural after what we all had done with each other. We walked up the hay field to the barn in silence. When we got there, Lida was wearing white shorts — tennis shorts, I think — but no blouse or anything else. It was hard to look at her and not look at her breasts.

"How's the water?" she asked us.

"We're going for a swim," Hollis said. He was in his swim shorts. "See you later."

We watched them walk down the field in the sun.

"I think they want to leave us alone. I think they want privacy," Erin told me.

I said I guessed the Lords were just acting natural, especially Lida. Erin began to smile but said I wasn't being funny. She pulled off her damp jersey and damp underpants and went out to drape them over the balcony rail to dry. The triangular remnant of sun that had lain at one end of the balcony was gone and a new bolt lay at the other end. Erin took one of the sleeping bags out there and unrolled it. I watched her naked in the sun on her hands and knees, smoothing the wrinkles, watched her lie down and turn her head away to rest her cheek on her folded arm. I lit the stove and began to heat a pot of water so I could shave. Erin got up, dragged the sleeping bag into the shade and lay down on it again. I wanted to tell her it was no good sunbathing in the shade and why didn't she get dressed, but of course I didn't say anything. I discovered I didn't feel like shaving and, furthermore, the stove was making the air hotter, so I turned it off. I wandered over to Hollis's shelf of French novels and took out the thinnest one I could find. It was called *Story of the Eye* and was supposed to be about eroticism and death, but even on the first page I came to words I couldn't translate, so I wedged it back on the shelf.

Erin was lying naked on the balcony, maybe asleep. I felt an uncomfortable flash of desire, but ignored it and opened my overnight bag and took out the mathematics conference booklet. Then I stretched myself on the floor and turned to the pages at the end where I had jotted some notes. The polished floorboards felt cool to my bare back, and I knew that the equations would be cool and restful, too. I intended to review the equations, but first I shut my eyes and set the open notebook on my face, so I could smell the paper and feel the smooth pages on my cheeks. After a while, I began to think about Erin and me and how strange it was that we had spent all our days and now our nights, too, with the Lords, and I tried to recall how it had come about. As far as I could tell, we had taken one logical step after another, day after day, until we had arrived finally at this craziness. The tight silken feel of Lida's body came back to me (when I had tried to pull out, she had said, "Don't. Nothing can happen. I assure you."), so now I tried to think about Erin, but all that came was a view of Hollis, his lean paunch and that heavy, swinging thing of his. I tossed the booklet and went out to the balcony. The sun had crept alongside Erin and had inched onto her buttocks. I leaned my elbows on the rail and squinted down the field. Hollis and Lida were sitting naked, side by side on a boulder in the sun, their feet in the water and a towel hanging from the tree limb behind them. I sat down in one of the canvas chairs, the last person on earth with his privates covered. "I'm hungry," Erin said behind me. "In fact, I'm starving."

We ate lunch sometime in the middle of the afternoon. On their way back from the pool, the Lords had turned to the overgrown vegetable patch and picked up and down the sprawling rows. Hollis came in carrying a towel filled with green peppers and celery, and Lida came close behind, an armful of tomatoes cradled against her bare breasts. "Pomodori," she said, spilling them onto the kitchen counter. She was in her white shorts, Hollis in his swim trunks. Erin came up, saying, "I can help with that." At least she had pulled on her underpants.

At lunch we talked haltingly of this and that, nothing close to us. Believe me, it felt strange, knowing what we all knew, to sit at the table and to look at Erin, her milk-white breasts, and to see Hollis with the gray in his chest hair, and Lida bare breasted, too, but you can feel strange for only so long and then the feeling wanes. Even our conversation smoothed out. Erin said she wondered what was going on in the outside world and whether we were at war again. Hollis talked about de Gaulle. I don't know how I wound up explaining why our little satellite and the big heavy Russian satellite had to travel at the same velocity if they were at the same altitude. Erin felt certain the heavy one should have to go much faster to keep from falling. Lida said she thought it was typical of the Russians to rocket a dog into space and then let it die out there. That's the way the talk went.

Then Lida started to put her hand on Erin's arm, but hesitated an inch away, saying, "I want you to understand, we want you to know that what happened today —" Then she faltered.

"We want you to know we didn't plan this," Hollis said, finishing for her. "Not the way you think, anyway."

"I know you think we tricked you," Lida said. "But we never had trickery in mind. We weren't carrying out a campaign. We had no strategies." A slight flush had come to her cheeks.

"The fact is, you two are likable, you're approachable," Hollis said.

"Let's be absolutely open," Lida said to him.

Hollis looked surprised. "What do you mean?"

"Tell them the whole truth," Lida said, her voice tense.

Hollis shrugged. "If you know the whole truth, tell it."

Lida glanced at me and Erin. "You're an attractive couple. You know what I mean. That night when we were all walking around in Albany, we, Hollis and I, we looked at you and we thought —" She interrupted herself to say, "First, you have to understand how much we like you."

Hollis came in quickly. "You were our past. We wanted to visit our past and maybe find where we had taken a wrong turn."

Lida ignored him. "We wanted to get close to you," she told us.

"How close?" Hollis asked her.

Lida flared at him, saying, "I never calculated how close! I never looked that far ahead and neither did you!"

"I thought you were going to be absolutely open," Hollis said.

"I *am* being absolutely open. Can you do it better?" she cried, throwing her empty hand at him, as if to show that she concealed nothing.

"These two people love each other," Hollis informed her. "I'm sure they've told each other everything. They're brainy. Maybe they know the truth better than you do."

Lida turned to Erin and said, "Did I ever mislead you? You knew I was interested in Bart. I told you so at the baths, remember?"

"Oh, yes, I remember," Erin said, becoming very still, her eyes on Lida.

"And I'm sure Hollis told you about it," Lida said to me. "You knew."

I started to speak, but there wasn't anything to say.

Lida turned back to Erin, saying, "And I told you how much Hollis liked you. We were in your room at the spa, talking about Bart and Hollis, and I told you how much Hollis admired you, wanted you. Remember?"

Erin sat rigid and watched her and said nothing.

"So everybody knew, before it happened," Lida concluded.

Everything began to slide away. I felt something like dizziness or nausea or suffocating desire, and I couldn't tell which. "Wait a minute. Hold on," I said.

"You make it sound as if we didn't know a thing!" Erin told her. She whirled up from the table, slid her plate rattling onto the counter, whirled around to face us, her breasts shaking. "The way you talk, it's as if you and Hollis did it all, seduced us, and we just went along without knowing where we were going. We knew. We knew everything."

"We're not dummies," I added, still feeling the vertigo.

"We did what we did!" she told Lida. "Jesus, Mary and Joseph! I'm not ashamed of myself and I wish you'd stop acting as if you ran the whole show."

Hollis's chin had sunk to his chest, his eyes skipping from Erin to me to Erin as we spoke. "Yes. Well. Who knows what the truth is?" he said, sitting up, taking a breath.

"Please, Hollis, don't get philosophical on us," Lida said, exasperated.

He barely shrugged. "Two people lie down together and twenty minutes later they get up with completely different versions of what happened when they were lying down."

"Now we're going to get the lecture on truth," Lida remarked.

"No," Hollis said. He turned to face Erin. "I never intended anything. I meant nothing personal."

"What do you mean, nothing personal?" Erin said. "Do you call going down on someone, nothing personal?" Her cheeks flamed.

I tried not to think.

"You're in love with Bart," he said, reasoning with her. "Bart's in love with you. You expect the world of each other. When I say nothing personal, I mean I don't want the world or anything else of you."

"Why fuck, if it means nothing?" Erin cried.

"I didn't say it meant nothing. I said I'd have it mean nothing *personal*."

"Stop it!" Lida told him.

"Do you understand this?" Erin asked her.

"Let's stop this right now before it goes any farther," Lida said.

"No!" Erin said. "I want to get this straight."

Lida took her dish to the counter and began to sort among the oranges and peaches there. "Come on, Erin. Don't waste your time. You know Hollis. All he means is, he doesn't want to interfere. Now let's drop the subject. Have an orange."

"But if it doesn't mean something personal, how can it mean anything at all!" she protested.

"I don't remember what we were talking about," Lida told her. "Come on. Let me rub your back, give you a massage."

"No. Don't touch me."

"Come on."

"No," she said, sullen.

"All right. How about you rub my back?" She took

Erin by the hand. "Please," she said, and led her away from the counter and out to the balcony.

14

I took my dish to the counter, picked up one of the peaches and began to peel it, my back to everything else. Hollis cleared the table, set the plates in the sink. I was torn up over Erin's making love with Hollis and at the same time I knew how nice and easy it had been for me to make it with Lida, and those two facts kept chasing each other around in my head. Hollis had gone to the ice box and now he came up with a tall green bottle of wine. He had difficulty with the corkscrew and when he poured the wine his hand trembled so much that the bottle danced and rattled on the rim of his glass. I could see he was coming undone but, frankly, I didn't care.

"Listen. I'm sorry. I really am," he told me. His eyes sagged down and I could see the red in the bottom eyelid.

"Oh, what the hell, Hollis."

"What? What are you thinking? Tell me." The unshaven stubble gave his jaw a light gray metallic glint, like iron.

"I don't know what I'm thinking. I'm too dizzy for that." I laughed but it came out more like a bark. "I don't even know what I'm feeling."

"Ah, Bart. You're like me. I mean," he added hastily, "I used to be like you. You think too much."

I started to laugh again.

"It's a fact. People who don't think always know what they're thinking." He brightened, smiled. "They have a certain difficulty in saying what they know, of course. That's why Eisenhower has trouble with grammar."

He had set a bowl-shaped wine glass on the counter for me and I witlessly dropped half the peach into it.

"That's good," he said, tipping the bottle to my glass. It rang so loudly I figured he had cracked the rim, but it stayed whole. "Peaches and wine is good. Good white wine, too."

"What do you think about?" I asked him

"Everything. Hadn't you noticed? In fact, Lida tells me I'm thinking myself to death. But all I'm trying to do is find out why we're so unhappy."

"Why did you say it meant nothing personal?"

He looked around for Erin and squinted painfully into the sun. "I was trying to be decent, Bart. I meant I didn't want to crap it up with biography or history. I wanted to keep it clean."

I didn't understand and my face must have showed it.

"You remember the woman in the black bathing suit, the one on the diving board?" Hollis went on. "We didn't know who she was, so we saw her with a special clarity. Right? There's a pure beauty that's revealed when the personal is left off, because then you have just the thing itself, no biography, no interpretation, just the thing itself, naked beauty. Understand?"

I said yes, just to get on with it.

"Because history is only the accumulation of mistakes and betrayal and filth," he told me.

At that hour the sun came flooding across the balcony and into the apartment, streaming over the golden floor boards, striking the walls and filling the room with light. Lida sat cross-legged on the floor in the sun, licking her fingers, a mess of orange pips by her feet and a corkscrew of orange peel around her wrist. Erin knelt down stiffly behind her and began tentatively to massage her shoulders. Hollis lifted two filled glasses from the counter, studied the trembling wine a moment, then carried the glasses across the room as if they might explode, handed one to Lida and set the other on the floor near Erin. He returned and took a fresh bottle from the ice box. "Plenty more. Drink up," he told me. I drained my glass, fished out the peach and ate it. Hollis refilled my glass. "One begins by loving the flesh," he announced.

"What?"

"For you and me, that means the flesh of a woman. Then one moves up the rungs to love the flesh of a woman who is beautiful, beautiful in many ways, then up more rungs to beauty itself, then truth, and so on."

"What's at the top of the ladder?" I asked.

"God, of course."

"Hollis got stuck on one of the lower rungs," Lida added.

Hollis went out to the balcony, but I lingered inside to watch Erin. She kept herself at arm's length behind Lida, her finger tips clutching the strong trapeze of muscle at the base of Lida's neck, rubbing and gouging it with her thumbs. I couldn't imagine that it felt good to Lida, but she closed her eyes and give herself up to the massage.

"Hollis has a lust for the absolute," Lida said quietly, her eyes still shut. "He used to go to a whore house in Venice and fuck his brains out trying to reach the absolute."

The way she had said *fuck* really jarred me. Hollis was standing at the balcony rail and without turning around he said, "Lida, I don't think anyone wants to hear this."

"I haven't got the story right," Lida told us sarcastically. She had opened her eyes. "In a dozen years I haven't been able to get it exactly right. — You tell it. It's your story," she called to him. Hollis didn't reply or turn around.

"So what happened?" Erin asked. She had stopped working on Lida's neck and took a long swallow of wine.

"Every couple of weeks he'd go to this Venetian bordello and fuck until he was exhausted. Sometimes he'd fuck one girl four or five times in one night, other times he'd take four or five girls one time each. The point was to fuck until there was nothing else left and then he'd know something."

"Four or five times?" I said, trying to make a joke of it.

"No one's interested, Lida." Hollis was still outside at the balcony rail, his voice mild, distant.

"I am," Erin said. "I'm interested."

"The concept was to do it until there was no person at the other end, just a pure fuck, and then he'd know what sex was or what it meant or something like that." She raked a hand thoughtfully through her hair a few times — the bracelet of orange peel still on her forearm — then tossed her head to settle the thick sheaves into place. "That's the part I never get right. It's pure, pure, pure theology."

"Oh, sure," I said, laughing. "Four or five times a night. That's some kind of story."

Hollis came in. "I was your age," he said.

"For Hollis, sex is the word of God made flesh," Lida told us.

"Then it's a word no one understands," Erin said, putting her glass gently on the floor.

"And for Lida, sex is just something practical and

useful," said Hollis.

Lida got to her feet, a bleak smile on her face, and went to the kitchen. She came back with the big shallow basket of oranges and peaches filling her arms. Maybe a story like that about Hollis should have bothered me, but the wine had begun to take effect and I felt relaxed for the first time all day. I refilled my glass. Lida had set the basket on the floor in front of Erin and the sun reflected from it to Erin's breasts and face, giving her a rosy flushed look. Her breasts were beautiful, and I felt sorry for Lida.

"How much did you know about this when you when you got married?" Erin asked her.

Lida looked over her shoulder at Hollis who had stretched out on his back on the sleeping bag, his trembling hand finally at rest upon his chest hair. "How much did I know, Hollis?"

"Everything," he said, squinting in the sun. "I believed in the truth in those days."

"Then why —" Erin had to pause because her mouth was full of peach. "Why did you marry him if —" She broke off to wipe her chin with her hand. The wine had reached her, too.

"Because Hollis was nice," Lida said, her voice flat, indifferent. "Hollis was decent. And the whole world was a mess. The war had been going on for ever. It was cold. The electricity didn't work. There wasn't any food. It had been horrible living in Trieste that winter, especially if you were living there on a Czechoslovakian passport. You never knew what was going to happen next. The partisans would kill one German soldier and the Germans would grab ten people off the street and shoot them. Then the Americans came and here was Hollis."

"To the rescue," Hollis murmured, his eyes half lidded against the sun.

"He was a nice clean American GI who brought us

canned food, and he knew how to talk about Byzantine mosaics and that satisfied my mother, because my father's specialty had been Byzantine icons. And when Hollis and I would go for a walk he'd talk to me about sex, but in an amazing way that made it sound grand and mystical." Then she sprang up and went off, saying, "I'm going to get the suntan oil."

Now I could look at Lida and Erin and see their breasts and not feel embarrassed or tense. I supposed it was the wine. Nothing in the room had changed but it seemed the air had ceased its shimmering vibration, as if a silent high-pitched alarm had stopped, and I saw the scene more clearly. The air was warm and soft and every now and again when I looked — if I let myself go completely when I looked — I could actually see the light in the air, just as you can see water and see through it, too, when the water is especially clear. Hollis had been talking about Trieste in 1945 and I hadn't been paying attention until just now.

"Because what Lida hasn't told you is that her mother had been having an affair with a major in the Italian army — for practical reasons, of course — but after the Italians surrendered he wasn't much use any more. In fact, he was a real liability. Because when the Italian army gave up the fight, the Germans turned on them and killed more Italian troops than we ever did."

Lida had returned and was on her knees in back of Erin, unscrewing the cap from the little bottle of suntan oil, a frown of concentration on her brow.

Hollis said, "So Lida's mother rigged up something useful between Lida and a Fascist Commendatore. The Germans and the Fascists still got along fine, so this was a good connection, this Commendatore — a distinguished gentleman, fifty years old, but quite vigorous. Lida was about twenty."

Lida swept the oil across the top of Erin's back, from

the tip of one shoulder to the tip of the other in a single, flat stroke of her palm.

Hollis said, "Might as well see the practical side of it. The right connections could protect them from the Germans. You just had to keep on making the right connections. The old Commendatore taught her how to fancy fuck and how to shoot a pistol."

"The Germans hanged people from the balconies in Trieste," Lida said, dripping oil into her cupped palm. "Hanged them by the neck from the balconies where everyone could see it. That's what the German soldiers would do."

"So it was practical, it was useful," Hollis said, concluding his speech.

Lida used both hands flat to rub the oil up and down Erin's glistening back, then she pressed her thumbs into the groove of the spine and slid them up to the nape of the neck. She tapped Erin between the shoulder blades and Erin leaned forward, pushed the basket of fruit aside, unfolded her legs, toppled down and stretched out on her stomach in the sun. Lida seated herself lightly on Erin's legs, against her buttocks, and began to work on her back in earnest.

I don't know how long I watched them. Hollis went away some place. Erin lay with her cheek on her folded arm, her eyes closed, and Lida never even glanced at me. So I took the time to look idly at the both of them, at the curious ways their bodies differed, and I drifted into a long daydream on their flesh, wondering if the big and little differences between their bodies meant something more than mere physical difference, wondering at the meaning of our bodies, these strange lovely hieroglyphs. Erin had turned over and had permitted Lida to rub her arms and shoulders and even the upper part of her breasts. Then Lida paused to rest and Erin sat up. Her cheeks were slightly flushed and she had a confused look, as if she had just awakened, and while she was draining her wine glass her nipples puckered and grew hard. I could feel myself getting loose, heavy. I unbuckled and stepped out of my trousers, but I kept my shorts on. At least I wasn't that drunk.

"How come you're still having sex with Hollis when you're getting a divorce?" Erin asked, her voice lazy with sleep.

Lida laughed briefly. She had taken an orange and was slowly pressing her thumbnail into it. "The sex has been better in the past six months than it's been in the past twelve years." She glanced up and smiled at us.

"I can't believe that," Erin said.

Erin's suntan oil had a pleasant scent. I put my hand on the nape of her neck and slowly shoved it up under her warm hair and she turned and brushed her cheek sleepily against my mouth. No matter the mess of bottles and glasses and dried orange seeds and velvet scraps of peach skin, it was easy for me to stretch out in the lassitude of the sun.

"And it wasn't bad during the twelve years, either. It's just much, much better now," Lida said.

"You make marriage sound sick," Erin told her.

"A good marriage means holding back a lot. And we had a good marriage. Marriage is built on not saying certain things and not discussing certain things. And if it's a perfect marriage, it means not even thinking certain things. We weren't perfect, God knows, but we were very good."

"I still don't see how you can go on having sex," Erin insisted. I had inched my shorts down enough to let this gross unmathematical thing lie stiff and heavy against the small of her back.

"Because it's never been better, Erin. It's that simple. Because divorce is all letting go. And when you let go you can really enjoy yourself and enjoy sex. I like it.

Hollis likes it. I hate to say so, but that's the way it is."

Erin made as if to shift herself to a more comfortable position, sliding her buttocks slyly against me, gratifying me and driving me wild at the same time.

Lida had made a long cut in the orange skin and now she studiously began to peel it. "We've let go of a lot of things. They were never worth hanging onto, but you don't know about that when you get married. Marriage means having to pretend you're a certain person, and divorce means you can let all that nonsense go. It's very relaxing. Or if you want, you can pretend to be anyone you want to be. That's a part I really like. We fuck and I can do whatever I want and be whatever I want."

"You?" Erin said.

"Yes, me. What's wrong with that? Didn't you ever play dress-up when you were a girl?" She looked at us and her gaze caught something and then she knew what Erin and I were doing.

The throaty sounds of German opera had been coming distantly from Lida's studio, and she murmured that Hollis was playing around with their ancient wind-up phonograph. "Hollis likes Wagner. It's his tragic flaw," Lida said, as if talking to herself.

She sank her teeth into the orange, watching us all the while. For I had pulled off my shorts and now I began to slowly peel down Erin's underpants. She lifted her hips and I rolled the underpants down past her knees and she kicked them off. Then she turned toward me as if she were melting in the heat of the sun and slid her knee over my leg. Lida passively watched us and remained sitting on the floor, her back against the door frame, one leg on the balcony and the other behind Erin. "You two are really a pair," she said, eating the orange. We didn't come together, but lay in that loose embrace I don't know how long. The sodden Wagnerian music from the studio had finally died. Lida stood up and pulled off her underpants and stretched out on her side, close behind Erin. She lifted Erin's hair and kissed her on the nape of her neck, but Erin shook her head, no. We let go of each other. Hollis had just come in. "What's going on?" he asked.

"Nothing," Erin said, sitting up and folding her legs aside.

I sat up, too, not that I could hide much.

"Don't mind me," he said.

"Ever make love while somebody was watching you?" I asked him.

"Not that I know of," he said.

Lida laughed and got to her feet and began to drink from one of the bottles, her head tilting back further and further, that thick swirl of pubic hair standing out.

"Has anyone noticed that the sun has stopped moving?" Erin asked, squinting at the horizon.

We all looked out across the balcony rail to the sun.

"It hasn't moved for the past half hour," Erin said.

"You're right," Hollis said, "And I hadn't noticed."

Lida handed the wine bottle to me and sat down. I caught the scent of orange and kissed her mouth and she put her arm around my neck, gently pulling me down. I was so overcome with desire I was shaking and at the same time I could hardly move. I tried to set the bottle carefully out of the way, but it whirled and bounced across the floor. Erin was watching us, her face attentive, almost severe. I turned my back. Lida's hand had closed on me and now she pulled me gently in and it was like sinking into a scalding bath. I drank in the citrus scent of her mouth and of the orange skins coiled around her arm. She drew her tongue slowly across the stubble on my jaw and then pulled her head back, doubling her chin, to look at me. There was a glaze of sweat on her cheekbones. Hollis had taken off his swim trunks. I had never seen a man's erection except my own and now I saw Hollis. I kept on looking out of rude curiosity at that alien thing, the sheath stretched so tight it shimmered in the sun, and all so heavy it sank and bobbed and swung as he walked. And there was Erin, her face as white as a sheet of paper, but unafraid, those watchful eyes and small flared nostrils. Her hand reached out for it.

15

I don't know how long we all lay there. The last time I came, I came hollow and dry and I collapsed and felt as if the marrow had been drawn from my bones. Eventually, Hollis got up and went to the little drawer where he kept the old photos of himself and Lida, but he didn't come back to show us any. Then Lida sat up and said, "Where did Hollis go?" I told her I thought he had gone out with some of those old photographs. She stared blankly at me, then yanked open the drawer so hard it crashed to the floor, spilling snapshots every which way. A moment later we heard her outside calling, "Hollis," and again, "Hollis." I saw him strolling naked down the hay field and heard Lida call his name again and now he turned and casually lifted his arm, as if were going to wave. He had the .45 automatic in his hand. He pointed it at Lida and she stopped walking. Then he turned away and began walking again and Lida began to trot after him. Erin was on her knees, peering out across the balcony at them. "Jesus, what's he going to do?" she whispered. I ran to the Lords' bureau, fumbled through the loose change and bills and address books, snatched up his car keys. "Let's get out of here," I said, pulling her up by the wrist. "Hurry." I pulled her out the kitchen door. *"We can't go anywhere naked,"* she whispered, jerking free. She ducked back inside. "Hey, Bart!" Hollis shouted.

My skin prickled and I could feel the hair on the back of my neck rise up. Hollis was standing in the middle of the hay field, looking at me, and the hand with the pistol was hanging loose at his side. I told myself he couldn't hit me from there. I got ready to drop. He could see the open door beside me, but he couldn't see Erin just inside, her hand stopped in mid air and her mouth open. Lida had halted about half way to him.

"Bart!" he shouted again.

"What are you doing?" I shouted back. My voice sounded strange in my ears.

"Do me a favor. Come here and get Lida," he cried.

"Why?" I didn't want to go down there. "What's going on?"

"Nothing. I just want to be alone to think." He closed his eyes, rubbed his brow with the back of his gun hand, then   looked   around   again.

I didn't know what he'd do if he saw I had the car keys, so I inched my hand behind my leg and let them slip to the ground.

"Hello, Erin!" he called.

"Hi," Erin called back, her voice dead.

She had come out the door, but I didn't dare take my eyes off Hollis to find her. "What the hell are you doing?" I asked her.

"I got scared waiting inside," she said.

I raised my voice to Lida. "Why don't we all back off?"

"You kids go inside. I want to talk to Hollis."

"I don't want to talk anymore!" Hollis shouted to me. *"Now get her out of here, will you?"*

"Hey, hey, take it easy," I said, alarmed. "Everything's all right." I tried to walk casually toward Hollis and Lida. He stood way off in the middle of the field, the brown grass up to his knees, one hand on his hip and his other hand down at his side with the .45 automatic gleaming at the end of it. There wasn't any sound in the world except for the small dry flutter of crickets whirring up and away from my foot steps. As I entered his range I found myself veering off to the right, away from his gun hand. Lida had drifted off to the other side and was standing with her arms folded, watching him. When we were close enough to talk, he said, "Thanks, Bart." His face was sweating.

"I'm not coming any closer," I told him.

"Just take her back to the barn," he said, nodding toward Lida. "I need to be alone." He sounded exhausted.

"I'm not coming any closer till you put down the forty-five. It scares me," I told him.

He stared at me a moment, suspecting a ruse. Then, as if to demonstrate that the gun had no particular purpose, he gave an exaggerated sigh and crouched down and laid it somewhere in the grass at his feet. He straightened up and looked at me. "There," he said, his chest heaving. "Now get her out of here. She's killing me."

But I didn't dare move. So there we were, the four of us, standing naked in the sweet horizontal light of the sun in the middle of the abandoned hay field. Erin was furthest away up the field. I was on this side of Hollis, and Lida was on the other side and closest to him.

"This isn't what you want to do, Hollis," said Lida. "You'll make somebody a good father, Hollis. Give yourself a chance."

"It's too late for that," he announced.

"Not for you. Not for you, it isn't," she insisted.

"It didn't work, Lida. We didn't get purified by them. It didn't work and there's nothing left to do."

"What do you mean? What's the matter?" I asked him.

"It's me," Lida answered.

"That's no reason —" I began.

Hollis cut in. "I know, I know. We should forgive each other. Let me tell you, Bart, we began our marriage by forgiving each other. Now you and Erin can try. Now that you have a few things to forgive each other for. See how you do."

"You know, Hollis —" I began.

"And please stop judging me."

"I'm not judging you."

"Sure you are. You both are. You look at me and what I've done with my life and you compare it to what you think you're going to do. You're convinced you're going to do much better. Old Hollis? He's a total loss."

"Come on," I said.

"And you're right! What have I got after all these years? Nothing." He hoisted his arms away from his sides to give us a better view of his nakedness. "Look. It all adds up to nothing. I've got nothing." He jerked his head down and about in a quick survey of his skimpy self, his lean chest and belly, limp prick. "Nothing at all."

"Hollis," Erin said.

"I'll tell you what it says, Erin." He looked at her and spread his fingers over his ribs. "I'll tell you what the body says. It says *we must die*. I'm dying, I'm dying! That's what the body says. I'm dying. No one listens."

"Why don't you wait till we're gone?" Erin said loudly. She had put a hand up to shade her eyes against the level sunlight. "We're leaving tomorrow morning, you know. Can't you wait till we've left?"

Hollis angry or maybe only astonished opened his mouth to answer, but by then Lida had already sprung forward and was in the air, her body seeming to elongate like the outstretched body of a cat pouncing on a bird, her legs and feet catching up just as her hands reached the nest in the grass where the gun had been. Because Hollis was faster. The startled gun seemed to have flown up and blundered into his hand, and he was already rising from his crouch while Lida sprawled. The gun fired — a flat CRASH, no echo. I was not hit. Erin wasn't hit. Lida stumbled up wildly. Hollis looked down at his feet, then looked around at us. "I'm shot. I'm shot," he informed us, as if he couldn't believe it himself. Lida stepped behind his hand and wrenched the gun from it, snatched out the cartridge clip and hurled it with all her might down toward the shadowy stream. "Ahhha!" Hollis gasped. Then he began to shout. "My foot. I'm *shot*. My foot! My foot!"

The .45 slug had smashed a hole through Hollis's right foot, just above the middle toe. We helped him hobble a few steps. Then I got under his arms from behind, Lida and Erin each took a leg and we stumbled up through the field to the barn. "Christ, I forgot we're all naked," I said. When we reached the door, Lida and Erin ran inside while I tried vainly to find where to press on Hollis's leg to slow the blood seeping from the wound. "It hurts," he said raggedly. "It really hurts." Erin dragged out a wood dining chair for him to sit on, Lida brought a couple of towels and pair of Hollis's under shorts and pants and a jersey. She wrapped his foot in a towel and held his leg out from the chair while Erin and I tugged his shorts onto him. Hollis was white and sweating. "We're not going to be able to get these pants on him," I said. Lida ducked inside, came out with scissors, hacked the bottom off the right pant leg. We tugged the pants up. Lida pulled the jersey down over his head, got his arms out properly, hauled it down over his damp torso. We threw on our clothes and seated Hollis slant-wise in the back seat of the car. Lida squeezed in beside Hollis and put her arm around him, Erin got in front (her shoes loose in her lap), I slid behind the wheel and started the car. "Take a right at the bottom of the hill," Lida told me.

"We have to have a story," Hollis said. "They report gunshot wounds to the police. We have to have a story."

"You were target practicing," Lida told him.

"Like last night," he said.

"We better get this right," Erin said.

"Target practice. Like last night," Hollis said.

"No, no," I said. "You went out by yourself. We didn't see it happen. You went out to practice. None of us saw it happen. We were all back at the house."

"You guys. Were back at the house," Hollis said. "Having a good time. Drinking and fucking around. While I was out there defending us against feet."

Erin laughed and said, "Oh, Hollis."

"Go right at the fork," Lida told me. A moment later she said, "He's fainted. I think he's in shock." She be-gan to sob. "He's going to die. Oh, God. Oh, God."

Erin turned around and knelt on her seat and held Lida's hand. I think they stayed that way until we ar-rived at the little hospital clinic. I pulled up to the emer-gency door, Erin jumped out and came back with two men who managed to get Hollis onto the stretcher, then Lida and Erin followed him inside while I parked the car. The light had been fading from the sky and now it was dark. A doctor and a couple of nurses gave Hollis intravenous infusions and worked to raise his blood pres-sure, cleaned his wound, x-rayed his foot to find bone fractures, and so on for a couple of hours. After he had been sedated and given a room, the three of us walked to a diner and ate a sandwich and drove back to the barn. We repeated to each other what the doctor had told us, that the immediate danger was past and that Hollis's condition had stabilized and there was no reason to think he would not make a good recovery. We were exhausted but no one was ready to sleep, so Erin made a pot of coffee and we stayed up talking quietly about Hollis, saying more or less the same things over and over. I don't know how many times Lida told us that no one else understood how decent Hollis was, but that there were terrible differences between them, irreconcilable differences, but that they loved each other, and that's why they had become so unhappy over the years. Maybe I was mindless from fatigue, for I was beginning to see the sense in what she said.

The next morning I got up early and shaved and went to wash off in the stream. Erin was there, toweling herself dry, and after my dunk in the pool we jogged back and ate a quick breakfast. An awkward distance seemed to be growing between the two of us, but maybe it was only because Erin was in her trim gray business suit again. "Let's all keep in touch," Lida said. She gave us her post office box number in the village and her address in Manhattan. And she didn't show any surprise when Erin and I exchanged addresses and phone numbers. I don't know if she was preoccupied with Hollis or if she had already figured out that Erin and I had really known each other only the past five days. Lida drove us to Albany. She dropped Erin off at the train station and me at Van Schaik's Foreign Automobile and Sports Car Repairs, then she herself headed back to the clinic.

16

I don't know when I began speeding. I couldn't find a place to park so I rode the VW onto the curb and ran across the street into the train station and raced over to the window where Erin had arranged her ticket. The ticket man told me no trains had left for New York in the last half hour. The next one was scheduled to leave in nineteen minutes. I ran downstairs to the platform, but the place was deserted except for a couple of baggage handlers. I ran back upstairs and looked around the concourse. It was a big place with rows and rows of oak settees, a few people sitting here and there, three people in line at a ticket window, one person at the magazine stall, two people at the coffee bar. I walked up the aisle and my heart began to thud, because I couldn't see her face but only the newspaper. It was last Friday's newspaper, the one she had bought at the news stand just before I swung my busted car around that monument and nearly ran over her. I said, "Erin." She turned and looked at me and it was as if she, too, were out of breath from running. "You," she said. It hadn't taken us long. The old newspaper sailed into the air every which way, then she picked up her leather portfolio and we walked out to the car and drove off.

That happened thirty-three years ago. After the divorce, Lida settled in New York City and Hollis moved out to the west coast where he had been looking for a job and eventually had found one as curator of prints and photographs in a new museum in the Bay area. As for me, I quit mathematics and went into linguistics, happy to find words messier and more ambiguous than numbers, and more satisfying, too. Numerals are all right for recording the date, but it takes words to recall what happened. I suppose that most of our remembrances eventually fall into a sort of dilapidation, a little detail drops off here and there, then some structural piece goes, and sooner or later the whole thing collapses, displaced by newer and brighter events. Three months ago I attended a conference on semiotics in Toronto and the return flight had a layover in Albany, so I rented a car and spent a day driving around, sightseeing the past.

There's no train station in Albany anymore, because they've ripped up the tracks and filled the huge stone structure with offices and shops. And they've knocked a big stretch of the city flat as a drafting table and built a long white marble plaza of State office buildings, white marble skyscrapers with here and there a huge stainless steel whirligig sculpture. About a mile away there's the old park with its stagnant gray lake, iron footbridge and lost Moses statue.

The town of Saratoga Springs looks more or less the same as it did thirty years ago. The hotel we all stayed at has been torn down, so I drove out to where the mineral springs and baths are located. They keep the lawns nicely mowed and the walks neat. The structures that housed the springs appeared to be in good shape from the path, but when I walked up to one I discovered that the portico floor was littered with chunks of stucco fallen from the ceiling, and the double-doors were chained and padlocked. They had turned one of the buildings into a museum of some sort and had closed down all the fountains and rotundas where you used to drink the waters, and I found only one bath building that was still working. The solitary attendant was helpful and gave me a sheet of paper with the hours and rates, and a list of all the minerals in the water. There wasn't much business, so he showed me around, leading me through the echoing foyer and down a hall of cracked plaster to a small room furnished with a chipped enamel chair, gaptoothed tile walls and a stone tub with a broad yellowish streak along the bottom. I tried to mentally repair the room so it would be like the one that Erin and Lida had shared, but I couldn't really do it. The attendant turned the water on full force and let me put my hand under it to feel its temperature. I thanked him for the tour, and as we were walking back he told me that the State of New York was in the process of refurbishing the park and that in a few years the spas would reopen and people would come back to take the waters and walk the paths and lawns, just as they had in the old days. I hope so.

Now Lida, she had kept in touch but in a haphazard fashion. A year or so would pass, then a large square envelope with a thick card inside would arrive announcing an exhibition of her work at such-and-such gallery in New York or Philadelphia or Baltimore, and sometimes the cards were signed and sometimes not. At first we used to write back to say congratulations and thank you, and we'd explain why it would be near to impossible for us to get down to, say, Baltimore for the exhibit, and Erin or I would end with a few lines about what was going on here at home, but Lida never acknowledged our letters and after a while I figured that we were merely names on a mailing list, names somebody had forgotten to cross out. We stopped answering.

Then one summer night we bumped into her at a gallery reception on Martha's Vineyard. That handsome woman of forty-five with lion-colored hair, the tanned face and a rolling laugh, yes, yes, that was Lida. It turned out we were not merely names on a list — she had read our letters and she remembered the names of our children and even what school grades they were in, but she wasn't a correspondent. She took Erin by the wrist and led us to the wall to meet her companion. "This is Bryant, my companion," she told us. Bryant was in his mid thirties, a good looking and diffident man who had kept his eyes on Lida throughout her conversation with us. We four chatted a while, then Lida turned privately to me and asked did I know that Hollis had remarried. No, I didn't know that. She had heard a rumor that he was about to quit his job at the museum, and she wondered what he was planning to do. I said I supposed I should have tried harder to keep in touch with Hollis, and maybe I would have if I thought we would ever meet again, but, well, anyway, I had not. "And you two?" she asked. "Are you living happily ever after?" I laughed and said "Yes." But it was 1968 and by then our lives had become richly entangled in ways too painful and foolish to unravel right there. She turned back to Bryant and told him, "Erin is the woman who held my hand all the way to the hospital the night Hollis nearly died." As Erin and I were leaving, we turned and saw Lida standing alone in the middle of the exhibition floor, watching us. We waved and she waved back — a striking woman in a sleeveless ultramarine dress. "She looks like the figurehead on a sailing ship," Erin said. "What did she tell you about Hollis?" I told her what Lida had told me. Erin always lingered over Hollis more than I did and liked to talk about him.

I laughed when Lida asked if Erin and I were living happily ever after, because the only true answer is *yes* and I knew that Lida wouldn't understand it. Years ago Lida had informed us that a good marriage required not discussing certain things, and a perfect marriage required not even thinking about them. Marriage means having to pretend, she had said. But it turns out that isn't true for everyone. For Lida, sex was something practical and pleasurable and she took pride in managing it well, whereas for Hollis it was the way to something beyond itself, a striving, a quest. I know they both regarded us as a couple of eager youngsters with the hots for each other, nothing more complicated than that. And maybe they were right. It's hard to remember how young we were, how full of easy energy and ignorance. But we were more knowledgeable and a lot less naive when the week was over. And there must have been moments when they saw themselves as a decadent and exploitive couple, preying on us young innocents. But Hollis and Lida were kinder and more generous than they knew. They laid themselves open to us, as if with a carving knife, saying, "See. This is what it looks like inside. This is the ailment, here and here. This is what we have become." The dark side of sex isn't in the silken gear we don or the whispered dramas we enact, but in the bitter histories we bring to bed. So it's good to know yourself, the swollen vanities and muscular willfulness of your lust, how easy it is to betray or be betrayed, how much or how little it matters, good to know ahead of time that your beloved is no angel, just a different kind of hairy beast when you get down to it. Our marriage is a complex affair (you get my meaning) and, yes, we're living happily ever after — yesterday and today and, with luck, tomorrow.

I know it's a rule of good literature that heady, dark erotic games should end in blood, especially when an older couple lures a pair of youngsters to play inside the labyrinth. But that's not what happened, unless you mean when Hollis shot himself in the foot. Lida continued to send us announcements of her exhibits and in later years we were able to attend some of her openings. She always had a companion with her, always a somewhat shy, good looking man. Her work began to gain acceptance and to sell better and by the late 1980s she became recognized, a face in the glossy art magazines (the sharp cheekbones, the eyes outlined in black), a personage at artistic and cultural events. "If they can't afford a Nevelson or Marisol, they come looking for me," she told us last year. Her companion, a man in his early forties, informed me that he was writing Lida's biography. That ought to be interesting.

As I said earlier, after the divorce Hollis had moved out to California to become curator of prints and photographs in a Bay area museum. We exchanged a couple of letters, but it wasn't much of a correspondence. He wrote a remarkably full, witty letter about the art scene in San Francisco and only in the last paragraph did he say anything about himself or that long weekend. He said he was still walking with a limp and that it got painful around four in the afternoon. *Of course I'm grateful to have come out of all that alive but I'm vain enough to wish I hadn't come out a damned fool. I really believed there was a way of looking at our bodies and how we do it that would reveal a meaning, and I still believe it — the disguises of love are not concealments, but ways to show our inner selves.* Later he sent me galleys of an article on Zen graphics he was preparing for a museum journal, and I wrote him about my prospective trip to Europe. After a lapse of two years I received a Christmas card (black pine bough, heavy snow) with a typed page folded inside saying he was living with a potter named Helen who had two young children, a girl and a boy, from a previous marriage. At the bottom of his letter he had penned, *We are so lucky to find each other in this vast world.* I mailed a belated Christmas card with a congratulatory note, but that was the last of our correspondence.

Lida sent me his obituary five months ago. The notice said that Mr. Hollis Lord died in Santa Cruz, California, at the age of seventy-five after a brief illness. An infantryman in World War II, Mr. Lord was awarded the Silver Star for bravery before returning home to become a museum director. In the late 1960s he left museum work and moved to a community south of San Francisco where he opened a commercial gallery, in later years widely known for its print workshops and its classes in Buddhist thought. He leaves his wife, Helen (Chen) Lord, and two married children, James Wu of Sacramento and Lillian Martinez of Oakland, and five grandchildren. The whole obituary notice was three inches long and there was no mention of a previous marriage.

That was a typical communique from Lida — a plain envelope addressed in her bold hand, containing a scrap of printed matter without date or signature. This scrap was only a photocopy of an announcement that had been cut from a magazine, an arts journal or an alumni bulletin or something like that, with no clue as to when it had been published or how Lida happened to have it.

"That weekend was thirty-three years ago," Erin said, still looking at it.

"How much do you remember?"

She handed me back the notice. "I haven't thought about it for a long time. But I can recall most of it. At least I think I can. I'm sure I can. I haven't made love to so many people I can forget them."

"We had sun all day every day."

"It rained one day," she said.

I said no. I didn't remember it raining.

"Yes," Erin said. "The day we drove from Saratoga to Albany it was rainy and we saw the accident and —"

"You're right. The old couple in the station wagon."

I asked her did she remember the name of that place in the Berkshires where the Lords had their barn. In fact, neither of us could recall the name of the town. But I remember as if it were only a week ago the four of us

standing naked in the sun in that upland field, and I recall the heat of the afternoon when we were walking
down the street, Erin and I, and I wanted her then and
there, and she knew my mind. I asked when her train
was leaving. "Twenty-five minutes," she said. She was
sweating and she tossed her head nervously again and
again, as if to shake the mane of black hair from her eyes.

A Note on the Author

Eugene Mirabelli lives in upstate New York and is the author of four earlier novels, as well as a number of shorter works. He is a founding director of Alternative Literary Programs in the Schools, a non-profit organization which brings poets and story tellers to the classroom. He also writes for a newsweekly focused on the arts.

A Note on the Type

The typeface used in this book is Adobe Palatino, designed by Hermann Zapf for the Stempel foundry in 1950. Palatino inherits its shape from Italian Renaissance letterforms; its large x-height and ample width make it highly legible, as well as graceful.